Glory of Love
by Sinclair LeBeau

Genesis Press, Inc.
Columbus, Mississippi

INDIGO LOVE STORIES are published by
Genesis Press, Inc.
406A 3rd Avenue North
Columbus, MS 39701-0101

GLORY OF LOVE

ISBN: 1-885478-19-4

Manufactured in the United States of America

First Edition

To my husband, Edward, whose love and support
is priceless.
To my children—Ted, Kevin, and Kimberly—who
mean the world to me.
To Sylvia, who guided and encouraged me
through this project.
To Wilbur Colom, for giving me the opportunity
to realize my dream. Thank you.
And in loving memory of my parents—Abel and Rosa—
who are always in my heart.

Visit our Web page for latest
releases and other information.

http://www.colom.com/genesis

Genesis Press, Inc.
406A 3rd Avenue North
Columbus, MS 39701-0101

Indigo Love Stories

Prologue

Fifteen years ago in Harper Falls, Virginia

"WHAT DOES NOT DESTROY YOU CAN ONLY MAKE YOU STRONGER"

"You didn't finish your chores last night, so you can't sit at my table for breakfast," Mrs. Fletcher snapped.

Nina Sterling stared at Mrs. Fletcher, her foster mother. Her fifteen-year-old eyes widened in disbelief. She couldn't figure out exactly how much she had to do to please the woman.

"I washed the dishes after supper last night. I did the laundry, and I pressed all four of Mr. Fletcher's uniforms like you asked," Nina responded. "I also helped the other kids with their homework. I had assignments of my own, but I didn't finish them. I fell asleep because I was so tired."

"But you didn't scrub my kitchen floor," the woman said. She waved off Nina's explanation with an angry toss of her

1

head. "I like my floor to be scrubbed clean every night." Mrs. Fletcher scowled at her.

"I swept it real good. I had only scrubbed it the night before," Nina explained. Her voice quivered at the woman's insensitivity.

"Every night. My kitchen floor must be scrubbed every night." Mrs. Fletcher turned her back on Nina to pour herself a cup of coffee. "You don't eat from my table until you scrub my kitchen floor. The chore is still yours when you come home from school today. Then you can eat my food." Mrs. Fletcher turned to face Nina and studied her with disdain.

Mrs. Fletcher was in her late fifties and weighed more than three hundred pounds, which she covered in tent-like, loud-colored cotton housedresses. Her short, badly tinted red hair didn't enhance her dark brown complexion; in fact, it made her appear more manly than feminine.

Nina's bottom lip quivered, but she lacked the nerve to tell Mrs. Fletcher what she thought of her. She had learned it was better to keep her feelings to herself. Otherwise, your life could be made even more unbearable by these state guardians. Nina crept out of the Fletchers' house. She hated Mrs. Fletcher, just as she had hated all the other guardians she'd been placed with since her mother's death three years ago. It puzzled her why these people always treated her like she was nothing. Despite their rudeness, she always tried to be pleasant to them. She stayed to herself and kept away from these people. She knew they didn't want to accept her as a part of their family, the way they were expected to. Her presence was only tolerated because of the monetary benefits they received to care for her.

It was at times like these that she missed her mother more than ever. At fifteen, Nina Sterling knew that there was nothing more precious than the love of one's parents. She observed other kids her age and listened to them whine and complain

2

about the restrictions placed on them by their parents. They'd whine about the way their parents nagged them to keep focused on their school work or pestered them to be mindful of their behavior, to maintain their self-respect as their character began to take shape. Nina had no one who cared about what she did with her life.

What caused these caregivers to dislike her so? Nina wondered as she made her way to Dubois High School with her stomach rumbling with hunger. Was it because she was plain-looking and sometimes rather clumsy, because she was nervous most of the time? Tears filled her eyes. She couldn't understand why she was treated like an outcast wherever she went. She couldn't help it that she had no relatives to care for her. She couldn't help it that she was a "welfare girl" who had to depend on these people until she turned eighteen.

After school that day, she headed for the Harper Falls Public Library. Her spirits were soaring by the time the school day ended. She had managed to get an A on her algebra exam and a B on a lab assignment in biology. Because of her free lunch ticket, she'd eaten a good lunch at school. That one meal would be enough to sustain her for the rest of day. She wasn't ready yet to return to the Fletchers', where she knew she would be attacked with verbal abuse. "Worthless" and "stupid" were labels Mrs. Fletcher had no qualms about attaching to the girl. Nina was not ready to be pelted with such hurtful words. She would hide out in the public library until it closed, she decided.

While Nina was in the library, she witnessed the arrival of some of the most popular seniors at Dubois High School. The guys and girls sat at one large table, smiling and chatting as though they didn't have a care in the world.

Nina pretended to study, but she watched the other kids, wishing she could be as carefree as they. Out of the six seniors,

Addison Wagner fascinated her the most. He was one of the best-looking guys she'd ever seen.

She had been aware of him from the first day the social worker had enrolled her at Dubois High. As a senior, he worked in the school office in the morning, during the homeroom period. Addison had greeted them with a smile when he had offered his assistance in showing them to the guidance office where Nina would get a class schedule. She had never forgotten the way he looked right at her that day and smiled. No guy had ever looked at her with such warmth. Looking into his brown eyes, Nina had thought they sparkled. Her heart had turned over, and she had been smitten by him ever since. She lived for the sight of him and his wonderful smile.

He had spoken to her a couple of times while she was at her locker, which had endeared him to her all the more. The simple courtesy flattered her and made her feel special. She wished that she looked better, dressed better, or even had the courage to engage him in conversation. However, she'd seen the pretty, vivacious girls who captured his attention. She was no match for them. Those girls probably came from good homes or lived in the same ritzy neighborhood as Addison.

Nina soon learned that Addison was the son of the wealthy Wagners. His father had his own successful law firm and served in the state assembly as well. His mother was gorgeous and very active in the community. Nina was fascinated to learn that Addison's mother had been one of the first black high-fashion models. His mother had come from money, too.

Seeing Addison around school, Nina noticed how well-liked he was by teachers as well as students. He was the kind of boy who drew people to him. His dazzling smile and his charm captivated whomever he spoke to. Because Addison served as president of the student government, he often spoke at the school assemblies. During the first assembly she

4

attended at Dubois High, she was mesmerized by Addison when he took the podium to make the announcements. He radiated charm, humor, and affluence without being pretentious. Most of the students in the audience gave him their rapt attention, because they respected and liked him.

She liked Addison a lot. He had become the object of her teenage fantasies. In her dreams, she had a chance to be the girl who was romanced by him.

While handsome Addison worked on an assignment in the library, an attractive girl sat on each side of him. They found reasons to lean close to him and to lavish him with teasing smiles while sharing textbooks or handing him notes to study.

Nina envied the girls who could talk to him with ease. She wished that she had the advantage of dressing like them in brightly colored, trendy outfits, or to feel light-spirited or giggly. It was unfair for her to be robbed of her adolescence by her unfortunate situation.

Although Nina had been at Dubois High School for nearly two months, she had not made any friends. In most of her classes she sat in the back of the room, trying to make herself almost invisible. In the other schools Nina had attended over the years, she had been the source of cruel jokes. She wore thick-lensed glasses and outdated clothes from the thrift store that were either too small or too large for her. Certainly no one wanted to associate with a loser like her, she reasoned.

The sound of soft laughter and the sights of the warm socialization from Addison's table made her heart ache. It would be wonderful to feel on the inside just once, instead of always feeling on the outside looking in, Nina thought. She frowned, trying to concentrate on an English essay that she needed to write. She figured that her good grades would be her passport to raise her above her grim existence. She refused to have her fate defined forever by her lack of a family.

By the time she left the library at closing, she found the October evening much cooler than when she had entered at three o'clock. She fastened the buttons on the unlined cotton jacket she'd been given to shield herself against the chill. As she descended the steps of the library, hunger pains roiled in her stomach. She thought of the kitchen floor and the supper dishes that she would be expected to do the moment she entered the door. And after all that work, she would only be given a bologna and cheese sandwich.

Walking slowly with her head down, she contemplated the angry confrontation that she would be drawn into by Mrs. Fletcher. She knew the woman intended to continue the argument over the chores she'd failed to do the night before. As she approached her neighborhood, she spotted two young men on the corner who had become a source of aggravation. They were in their late teens, and deadbeats. They spent most of their time hanging out on the corner, begging loose change from passers-by for cheap wine or drugs. When Nina was sent to the neighborhood store, she'd often see them. They never missed an opportunity to utter sexual innuendoes to her when they saw her.

"There she is. Our little welfare girl," exclaimed the heavy-set boy with a light complexion, sidling up beside her.

"What's up, baby? We've been waiting for you all day," the taller, thin, dark one said as he fell in step on her other side.

Her heart pumped with anxiety and fear. She refused to acknowledge them by saying anything. She kept her gaze away from either of them and clutched her books to her, hoping they would leave her alone.

Suddenly the night became more ominous. The two tough guys crowded her as she turned and walked down the deserted street into pools of darkness. She felt as though she and the two thugs were the only people who existed in Harper Falls at this horrible moment.

"Why won't you say anything, baby?" the heavyset one said, stepping in front of her. "Don't put on airs with us. You of all people can't think you're too good to talk to us." He puckered his lips at her as though he wanted a kiss, then he laughed. "Everybody knows what mean rats those Fletchers are to the kids they keep. I had a buddy who lived there, and he hated them so bad that he ran away and lived on the streets."

Looking into his menacing face, Nina knew that there would be no reasoning or pleading with him until they did something horrible to shame her. Both of them had been in and out of detention homes at various times for shoplifting, burglary, and assault. On several occasions, she had seen them fondling girls her age for sport. Tears began to well in her eyes. She attempted to walk around him. They were not going to harm her without a struggle.

The tall one yanked her arm and pulled her to his side. He knocked her books out of her hand. He snatched off her eyeglasses and held them behind his back, then laughed cruelly at her futile attempts to get them back. "She looks a little bit better, but not much, man. But then, she doesn't have to be a beauty queen for what we've got planned."

Fear gripped Nina's heart like a cold hand. Please, God, let someone save me from this nightmare, she thought, paralyzed by the impending horror she was certain would come.

The heavyset creep darted around behind her, then grabbed her. He cupped her breasts and squeezed them while he pulled her roughly against him. "She got some nice hooters, man. I can't wait to see them." He laughed in Nina's ear.

"Let me go! Please, leave me alone!" she cried, her face washed in tears.

"Let me go." The tall boy mimicked her whiny voice. "We can't do that. My man and I are about to do you a little favor.

7

We're going to do something that no other man will do for a mousy nobody like you." The tall one moved in front of her and grabbed the lapels of her jacket, tearing it open. The heavyset guy held her arms so that his buddy could tear at her clothing and slip his hand up under her sweatshirt to feel her bare breasts beneath her bra.

The harsh feel of his cold, groping hand made Nina cringe. Her breath seemed to have solidified in her throat.

"Yeah, baby. You're going to love us before the night is over." He unsnapped the front of her jeans and ripped the zipper down to slip his hand inside her panties.

Nina folded her body forward to keep him from touching her genital area and struggled to get away. Fear, stark and vivid, spiraled through her.

"Help me control this b*@*#," ordered the heavyset boy, finding it difficult to hold on to Nina. "I'm tired of her playing hard to get."

"Let's just carry her to that old vacant house on the corner. We can work her like we want there, man," said the taller boy.

He hooked Nina under one arm while the other guy did the same on the other side. Nina dug her feet stubbornly into the ground, making it difficult for the thugs to drag her away. One of them slapped her twice across the face. His action terrified her. It rendered her weak and frightened enough to be dominated.

"Help! Stop it!" she screamed hysterically. She struggled against their strength. Her efforts were useless. Clutching her arms more tightly, they dragged her in the direction of the house they had spoken of.

How much more humiliation could she bear? Ever since she had begun to develop, she had had to fight to maintain her virtue. She had to leave the last foster home she was in because the brother of the lady she lived with had fondled her and kept offering her money to have sex with him. That awful man had scared her half to death one night when he slipped into the bathroom while she was showering. When Nina had revealed this situation to her foster mother, she wasn't believed. The woman had called Nina a liar. Her brother was a deacon and a faithful worker in the church, her guardian had said. He was also a good husband and father. The woman had accused Nina of being a hussy, because her brother told her that Nina had offered him sex for money on several occasions. Nina had been whisked away from that place and dumped at the Fletchers. And here she was again, fighting with young men who wanted to humiliate her by violating her body.

Hearing the constant blaring of a car horn coming from the curb, the boys froze in their attempts to hustle her away for sex. They exchanged nervous glances.

"Oh, damn!" one of them exclaimed. They glanced in the direction of the car with its interfering horn. They shoved Nina to the ground as though she were a rag doll. They fled, disappearing into the night down the first available alley.

Dazed and in shock, Nina found herself on her hands and knees, scrambling to gather her books and her eyeglasses.

"Let me help." A kindly voice spoke. A man knelt to help her. He stacked her things, then extended his hand to her.

Nina cowered in fear. She was reluctant to accept this man's hand. Was he only setting her up to humiliate her too?

"Everything is all right. Those creeps are gone," he said. "I'm Addison Wagner. I remember you from school. You're that new girl in the freshman class."

Pulling her torn jacket around her, Nina burned with shame. She must look a sight to this guy who was always clean-cut and smiling as though he never had a care. She was embarrassed that he had to see her at her worst. Her hair hung in a tangled mess. Her face was washed in tears. She dabbed unhappily at her nose, choking on her misery.

"I was so scared. They . . . they were going to rape me. I just know it." The horrific what-ifs made her tremble. She was fortunate Addison had appeared when he did.

"It's okay, really," he assured her. "We'd better get out of here, though. I can't fight both of them off if they come back." He glanced over his shoulder and once more extended his hand to help her off her knees.

She accepted his offer. The moment she placed her hand into his, her heart swelled with gratitude at his kindness. There was no telling how badly those guys would have ravished her had Addison not come along when he did.

"I'm going to take you home. You're safe now," he said, resting his arm on her shoulder in a comforting manner. He gave her a warm smile and led her to his sleek, stylish car; he helped her inside with care.

"What's your address?" he asked, handing her his handkerchief to wipe her tear-stained face.

"Make a right three blocks from here," she murmured, wiping her eyes. "I live at the second house from the corner."

He followed her instructions and eased his car in front of the Fletchers' house. He hopped out of the car and ran to her side to open the door.

Despite the situation, she took note of his kindness. She'd never had any man treat her this way. It made her feel simply wonderful to be respected by someone like him.

As she exited, he took her hand once more and then handed her her books.

"Thanks . . . thanks so much." She managed a smile.

"I didn't do anything. I'm glad you're all right. You need to tell your folks. They'll probably want to report it to the police or something."

"Yeah . . . I'll tell them," she said. She was certain that the Fletchers probably wouldn't care about what had happened to her.

"I'll wait in my car until you get inside," he said. "Good night."

"Good night."

Once Nina reached the porch of the house and rang the doorbell to get in, she turned and waved to Addison.

He nodded in satisfaction and pulled away the moment he saw Mrs. Fletcher open the door.

"Where in the world have you been, girl?" Mrs. Fletcher was in her face. She anchored her feet and placed her hands on her huge hips.

Nina shrank away from her. "I . . . I've been in the library. Studying."

Mrs. Fletcher looked her up and down, taking in her torn clothes and the tangled mess of her hair. "Did this happen to you in a library?" She angrily grabbed the front of Nina's tattered jacket.

Nina burst into fresh tears. "On . . . on my way home, two boys grabbed me. They tried to . . . to rape me."

Mrs. Fletcher glared at her. For a moment Nina thought she believed her. Just once, she thought, she was going to offer some sympathy or show some kindness to her.

Her hopes were dashed by Mrs. Fletcher's next words. "The social worker warned me about you and your lies. You've been out there whoring around. That's something I won't tolerate. I'll turn you back in. I refuse to be worried with a girl who is hot in the tail." She pointed her finger in Nina's face. "You knew those chores were waiting for you. Well, your lies won't keep you from doing the work that's waiting." She grabbed Nina by her shoulders and shoved her toward the kitchen. "Get busy. I'll be waiting up for you to make sure you do everything

11

you're supposed to. You worthless, stupid slut!" she hollered. She stomped out, leaving Nina alone in the cluttered, messy kitchen.

Nina laid her books on the kitchen table. She leaned on the table and allowed the pain and the humiliation of the entire day to wash through her. Her body shook with her hard sobs. Through her tears, she spotted the folded white handkerchief Addison had handed her, resting between her books. She picked it up, dabbed her eyes, and wiped her nose.

When she smelled the soft scent of his cologne, a tiny smile tilted the corners of her mouth. Addison was the first person to be kind to her in a long time. He was like a knight in shining armor, protecting her honor and treating her like a real lady, not the worthless welfare girl who had to face the cold, cruel world alone.

Addison would always be her hero. She'd never forget his kindness.

Chapter I

Where the devil was he?

It was eight o'clock in the evening, and the crowd at Finnegan's Steak and Ale Restaurant was lively. Dr. Nina Sterling sat in a corner booth alone, drinking coffee to fight off her weariness. She pulled off her thick glasses, rubbed her eyes, and sighed. So much remained to be done for the upcoming festival to benefit the Family Free Clinic. Nina wanted it to be a success—not only because it had been her idea, but most importantly, because it would serve as additional revenue for the clinic that helped so many people in the black community.

To kill time, she'd read over the notes from the meeting that had dispersed twenty minutes earlier. She'd just about decided to leave; then she peered out the window and saw her tardy colleague, Dr. Addison Wagner. He pulled into the restaurant parking lot in the sleek Porsche that befitted his playboy reputation. She watched him as he exited his car, looking like a Hollywood celebrity. He added elegance to simple blue jeans and a khaki-colored shirt, she mused.

13

He strolled toward the restaurant with his usual long, proud gait, in that unique manner he had of always holding his head high with his shoulders squared confidently. Anyone checking him out could see that he was in no way one of those brothers who lacked self-esteem or pride. Unlike most women, who only admired Addison's good looks and nice physique, Nina thought his sense of pride and his confidence were the most sexy qualities about him. However, she would never let him know. He had enough women fawning over him as it was.

Nina remembered how enamored she used to be of Addison. They had both attended the same high school. Addison was a charmer, sweet and sensitive. She had never forgotten how he had saved her from what could have been a terrible crisis. He had been her hero.

He had never been aware of how much she thought of him after he had come to her rescue. After that incident, they'd only exchanged quick hellos and nothing more. He had graduated that year, and she had not seen him again until she returned to Harper Falls to practice medicine and work at St. Luke's Hospital.

During her first week at St. Luke's, she had been pleased to find that Addison was also a physician. When he had approached her in the lounge to say hello, Nina had beamed. Surely he remembered her after all these years, she thought. It wasn't until she mentioned Dubois High that she realized he had no memory or clue as to who she was. Nina Sterling was a new physician he was welcoming to the staff; nothing more. She had been crushed. Yet she had to accept the fact that at that time, Addison's senior year, she was one of the most forgettable students in school.

By the time he sought her out in the restaurant, she pretended to be lost in her reading. "Where is everybody?" he asked, taking the seat opposite her.

"They went home. We've been here since six-thirty. We

accomplished a lot, and could have done more had you shown up in time with your report." She stared at him, trying not to be affected by his wonderful, luminous eyes.

"I thought you said this thing was at seven-thirty," he said, signaling for a waitress.

"At either time, you're still late. And where is your report with the figures I need?" she asked. He angered her by expecting to place an order, as though feeding himself was the most important item on his agenda! He had not apologized for being late, nor had he bothered to even ask what was accomplished at the meeting.

"It's at home," he said calmly. "I haven't been there all day. I came here from the gym. I'll get it to you tomorrow sometime. You want to fill me in on what went on?" He rubbed his ear and looked around as though he really didn't care.

"I shouldn't tell you anything. Addison, you haven't shown the other members of the committee much respect by being so cavalier," she flared. "You and I are the only professionals. So why can't you act like one? You've only made it to half of our meetings, and you've been late for those."

"I've been pulling my weight. I don't have the time or patience to sit and listen to banter about what color to make the t-shirts or the caps to be sold. The one meeting I sat in on with you girls, you spent the whole time disagreeing over the color and logo for that stuff."

"That's not so! You're just pissed because you're the only man on the committee and we won't let you make all the decisions."

"That's not true," he responded tightly. "Lady Chairman, you told me you wanted me to be in charge of arranging the number of concession stands and engaging the talent to perform for that day. I've taken care of that. It's all arranged. Okay?" His annoyed expression eased into a smile for the young waitress who set a cold beer before him. "Could you bring me one of those fabulous burgers this place is famous for?"

Nina watched the young girl blush from his disarming smile as she took his order. It was shameful the way he used that smile and a wink to maneuver women, she thought in disgust. He could be forgiven anything with that charm of his, and he knew it and overused it. To see him in action irritated her. She hated to see any woman manipulated in that way.

"I'll be glad when this is over," he said after the waitress left. "You've been in a tizzy ever since you started organizing this grand event of yours."

"I have not been in a tizzy," she snapped. "Whether you want to believe it or not, this will be a very important event. I don't appreciate your putting down my efforts. I'm sorry I even asked you to work on the committee. But when you consented to do so, I thought maybe you had some genuine interest. Had I known you were going to bring your country-club values, I certainly wouldn't have involved you!" She rubbed the back of her neck to alleviate the tension she felt.

"I'm pulling my weight," he said coldly. "It might not be to your liking or your frenzied style, but I'm making my contribution."

"It's pointless discussing this with you now. Everything will be over with in a few weeks." She glanced away from him and gnawed her lip nervously. She didn't know why she nagged him more than she did the others. There were others on the committee who hadn't worked as hard as he. Was she using her little authority for the festival to get extra attention from him? Before, when they'd worked at the clinic, Addison had had very little to say to her on a personal level. Could it be that she still harbored a school-girl crush for him? Could she still be dreaming that he would look at her and see that she secretly adored him behind her cool, professional attitude?

"I'm still not confident about this," he said. "I think you made a mistake by tagging it as an African-American thing. It might discourage other people in the city from participating. We should have called it the Harper Falls Summer Festival, as I suggested."

"I don't agree. I was interviewed by a news reporter just yesterday, and I made it clear that it was open to anyone who was looking for a fun-filled and interesting day. There are so many other events that take place in the community where our ideas and talents are excluded. This will be just our day to show our pride and our talent. We'll also be letting Harper Falls see that we do support each other and that we are not always looking for a handout. It's going to be a gorgeous day for all of God's children to get together."

"Preach, my *sistah*," Addison teased.

"I wasn't preaching, my *brothah*." She glared at him. "I'm only trying to show you how to keep it real."

"Oh no, here you come with that 'keep it *real*' bull. Are you trying to insinuate that I don't have any black pride?"

"Let's just say you have no idea what it's like to go without, as a lot of us have had to do. You've been insulated from a lot of the grim realities of what it's like for most blacks."

Addison's face became tight and pinched. "Don't start that, Nina. I'm a black man, and I don't try to be anything else but that. My experiences may be different, but they're my reality, and you can't make me ashamed of what my family achieved." He heaved a sigh. His vexation was evident. "I'm quite aware of what goes on. I work in that free clinic with you. I've talked to the patients, and I see their pain. I empathize with them."

"Yes, but you walk away from it every day and forget it. You can go off to your fancy gym to work out or escape to the golf links for relaxation to forget the problems of our indigent patients. You haven't a clue of what it's like to live without heat

17

in the winter or not to have enough money to feed your kids or give them the proper medication or medical care."

Addison's ire over Nina's lecture turned to relief when the friendly waitress appeared and set his order of burger and golden fries before him.

"Perfect," he told the young lady, making an okay sign to her with a soft chuckle. "Have some?" he offered Nina as he squirted catsup on his fries.

"No, thank you," she responded sardonically. "I really should be going. I have some things I need to record in my computer for this affair." She reached for her purse and dug for her car keys.

"Don't leave. Stay and keep me company. I hate eating alone." He winked at her. "However, I'd appreciate it if you wouldn't preach while I'm eating. Why don't you have a glass of wine? You need something to relax you."

Nina relented. A glass of wine did appeal to her and her jagged nerves.

"You should have a date waiting for you tonight," Addison said, before he took a hearty bite of his burger." You shouldn't devote your entire weekend to this thing. An evening with some lucky guy could remove the stress on your face and the way you've been dragging around lately."

"I don't need a man to energize me, thank you." That comment coming from him embarrassed her. She felt a warm flush on the back of her neck. She sat tall in her seat to improve her posture and wondered if she looked haggard. She tried to dismiss Addison's criticisms. She knew he was only trying to swipe at her for the way she had gotten on his case, concerning his aloof attitude.

He munched on a couple of catsup-drenched fries and gazed at her with a hint of mischief in his eyes.

She glanced away from him, letting her gaze stray around

the room to break the spell of his charm. His scrutiny heated her. She hated the way her body betrayed her around him. She knew she looked a mess. She had been up since 3 A.M., delivering a baby to first-time parents. What with her work at the clinic, her private practice, and attending to the details of the festival, she hadn't taken time to go to the beauty parlor. She needed to have her hair trimmed. She needed a perm. Then she chided herself for allowing him to make her feel self-conscious. Why should she care what he thought of how she looked?

Her eyes wandered to his mouth and the way he ate his fries and licked the dabs of catsup off them. She looked down at her papers to hide her interest in his sensual mouth. His lips were smooth-looking and slightly full. Her curiosity was piqued. They were very nice lips. Was he a good kisser? she wondered, returning her gaze to his with a hint of a smile. She brushed the thought from her mind. Her smile faded and she cleared her throat. She wasn't about to be bewitched by this arrogant cuss. Her feelings wouldn't be appreciated by him. Nor did she want them to be by the self-centered man that Addison had become over the years.

"Didn't your mama tell you it was impolite to stare?" he asked with a grin.

"Yes, she did. Excuse my manners." She smiled and broke their stare to sip her wine. It's his eyes, she mused. Whenever he looks at me a certain way, he makes me dislike myself for not being his kind of woman. He fuels those dreams I've been trying to let go of for so long.

"I was just thinking you're too young to be without a man in your life," he said. "I was wondering what you're afraid of."

"I'm not afraid," she snapped defensively. "If I'd allowed myself to be distracted by the foolish games men play, I wouldn't have been able to do the things I've done. I've seen too many bright women lose sight of who they are and what they really want to do because they thought having a man validated them more than having a career."

"Get out of here," Addison said. He laughed. "You are one serious woman. Boy, do you need to lighten up." He shook his head. "You don't have to sacrifice your life to go out on a date and have some fun."

"Well . . . I don't have time to date." She squirmed in her seat. Could it be that he wanted to ask her out to smooth things over between them? She wouldn't mind at all being his date for an evening. Her heart raced at the thought.

Just then he glanced toward the entrance of the restaurant, and a broad grin slashed his handsome face.

She turned to see what had captured his attention. An attractive, cinnamon-complexioned young woman close to Nina's age came toward them. Her hair was cut stylishly short, emphasizing her oval-shaped face and wide eyes. She wore a two-piece floral print mini-skirt outfit and carried an oversized tote bag. She came up to Addison. He stood to greet her with a kiss and patted the chair beside him. Nina's ego deflated as her dream of a date with him vaporized.

"Nina, this is Mia Keaton, from New York. Mia, this is my colleague, Dr. Nina Sterling." He smiled broadly at Mia.

"Pleased to meet you," Mia said brightly before turning her attention to Addison and rubbing her shoulder against his. "Is that meeting over with?" she asked, crossing her shapely legs.

Nina felt like a wilting flower next to the woman who sat close to Addison and stared at him as though he were the only person in the restaurant.

"Yes. It's over. Nina was just keeping me company until you came." He eyed Nina sheepishly.

Mia leaned toward him, giving him a secret look. "So, what are our plans for the evening and what's left of the weekend?"

"I have a couple of things in mind." He took Mia's hand

and squeezed it. He ignored Nina as though he had forgotten she was there. "I've just eaten. Would you like me to order something for you, Mia?"

"I'd love a salad and some iced tea. I've been rushing all day to get to you. I came straight here from the airport, as you suggested."

"It's yours, sweetheart." He signaled for the waitress. "Uh ... Nina, can I order something else for you? My treat."

"No, thank you. I'm leaving." Nina gathered her things and rose to go. She felt dowdy in her denim jumper and a white t-shirt. "I hope I can count on you to give me the final report on your assignments for the festival."

"Of course," he said. "You have nothing to worry about."

"Nice meeting you . . . Mia," Nina said. "Good night, Addison."

"Yeah. Okay." Addison acknowledged her good-bye with a quick wave. He and Mia leaned close together, talking softly and laughing.

"Addison, you're such a bad boy." Mia squealed with delight—loud enough for Nina to hear as she turned to leave.

Outside in the summer night, Nina couldn't believe his nerve. He'd arrived at the meeting late and had shown up without his part of the report for the festival. Then, to top things off, he had arranged to meet his weekend interlude when he should have been showing interest in the festival. But then again, she shouldn't have expected too much concern from him. Addison Wagner had had everything his heart desired his entire life. He couldn't really relate to how important the free clinic was to the people who really needed the assistance.

When Nina reached her car in the parking lot, she turned to look back through the window of the restaurant. She could see Addison and Mia. She saw them share a brief kiss. It aroused envy within her, and a deeper sense of loneliness than usual.

Chapter II

Getting out of her white, two-year-old Honda near the blocked-off streets of downtown Harper Falls, Nina Sterling squinted up at the blazing sun and blinked with the unfamiliarity of her new contacts. She'd had them for a few days, and still hadn't fully adjusted to them. She was wearing them today to give her more freedom to relax. Her heart bubbled with excitement at the sights and the sounds of the event. So what if the July day was sweltering? she thought, wiping perspiration from her brow.

Despite the smothering humidity, she was pleased to see the turnout for the first African-American Festival of Harper Falls. The Family Free Clinic was sure to receive a whopping donation from the activities of this event. All the hard work and frustration she'd been through had been worthwhile. She couldn't wait to see Addison. Although he had gone through the motions of supporting her, she could tell that he considered her festival idea foolhardy. Looking at the full parking lots and the number of people still pouring into the fair lifted her spirits. She couldn't wait to see Addison eat humble pie.

The downtown area swarmed with people listening to music, ranging from rap to reggae to jazz to oldies-but-goodies of the rhythm and blues era when music was sweet and sassy. The air filled her nostrils with the tempting odor of hot dogs, hamburgers, barbecued chicken and seafood, and other ethnic dishes of the South. Vendors hawked t-shirts with colorful prints of African-American heroes and motivational phrases.

To support the cause behind this fabulous day, Nina had ordered several of the t-shirts that were being sold. One displayed a cluster of black women of different hues dressed in red, green, and orange. The saying beneath it read, "Sisters in the Name of Love Accomplish Great Things." The other shirt was light blue, commemorating "The First Annual Harper Falls African-American Festival—A Benefit of Love."

Strolling along Skylar Boulevard, which was pleasantly crowded for the event, she met several of her patients. They waved and called out to her with warmth; one young woman stopped her to show off the kids that Nina had delivered.

"This is Malik, who will be two years old, and this is LaDonna, who will be six months," Monica Cason said with pride. "And this is my mother-in-law, Mrs. Velma Cason. She is visiting us from Atlanta."

"Pleased to meet you, Dr. Sterling," said Mrs. Cason. "I've heard so much about you. When Monica told me you delivered her babies, I couldn't believe it. You look like a college girl." She grinned at Nina.

"Mama Cason, you're embarrassing Dr. Sterling," Monica said.

"No need to apologize." Nina lifted her ponytail off her neck with a flip of her hand and smiled. "I get that a lot. I'm usually mistaken for a candy striper or a clerk by people at the hospital who don't know me. You should see some of the fathers when they first meet me. The look in their eyes lets me know that they are skeptical of my qualifications for being a real ob-gyn doctor."

Monica and her mother-in-law chuckled. Mrs. Cason continued to scrutinized Nina as though she were a wonder.

Dismissing the amazed look, Nina knelt to get a closer look at her kids—the ones she had delivered. She took a reluctant Malik's hand and shook it. "You are one handsome young man." She smiled at him. "And she is simply lovely, Monica," Nina said, palming the side of baby LaDonna's chubby face.

"We did a good job, didn't we, Doc?" Monica laughed.

"We sure did. I'm so proud of you. You've lost all that baby weight. You're looking good." Nina gazed at Monica with approval. "I wish all my patients took as good care of themselves as you did during your pregnancies."

"I had good care with you. You removed a lot of the stress during those months. You were always available and always took all of my questions seriously, no matter how silly they were. That meant a lot to me, especially when I had my first."

"Having babies has changed so much since I had my children," Mrs. Cason said. "For one thing, there weren't any women doctors around to care for my generation. I would have loved to have a woman doctor to discuss my female problems when I was younger. When I carried my kids, you just did as your doctor told you. And you didn't challenge him concerning your care."

"I hear that from a lot of my patients. It's nice to have a choice now, isn't it?" Whenever she saw healthy kids like Malik and LaDonna that she had helped nurture and bring into the world, Nina felt a surge of pride. "Are you having fun?" she asked the two women.

"It's simply marvelous," declared Monica's mother-in-law.

"It's about time Harper Falls had something like this for blacks in the community. There was nothing like this when I lived here before moving away. Sharing our culture can be so beneficial. So positive."

"It's a wonderful way to spend the day with the family. I hope this becomes an annual event," Monica said. "There's so much to do and see. As soon as we can locate my husband in this crowd, we'll be on our way to the area set up for the kids. Malik heard about the pony rides, and that's all he's talked about since we arrived."

"I'm pleased you're having fun. I have to let the people who are responsible know this. It was nice seeing you and your kids, and meeting you, Mrs. Cason." Nina extended her hand to the older woman. "Don't let those kids eat too much," She reminded Monica good-naturedly as they separated.

Stopping at a jewelry booth, Nina eyed the sterling silver necklaces and the uniquely styled dangling earrings with interest. She thought of buying a pair, but decided they would look foolish on her. She was more conservative. Besides, she didn't go out often enough to wear the dazzling and fun earrings that most women wore with confidence.

"Get something fly."

Nina turned to see who had spoken. It was Jenny Martin, one of the clinic volunteers and an old childhood friend.

"These would really be ideal for you." Jenny eased up beside Nina and held a pair of large wire double-hooped earrings against Nina's face. "Since you have contacts now, you can wear any style of earrings."

"That's not me," Nina said, frowning at Jenny. "No, that's not me. They're a little too much for me. I still use my glasses at times. I haven't gotten completely comfortable with these contacts yet." She noticed Jenny's trendy, large golden earrings in the three holes in each of her earlobes—a bit much for Nina's taste, but wonderful for Jenny. It suited her flair for being with the latest trends.

Nina wasn't into trends. To her, they were a waste of money. What looked great on most women would only come off looking ridiculous on her, she decided. It was best that a plain woman like herself stick to the basics when it came to clothes. She'd had her share of being the butt of bad fashion jokes because of what she'd had to wear growing up.

"Where's my hug?" Nina directed her attention to Jenny's daughter, Chloe, and scooped the giggly little girl into a bear hug. "Have you pulled your shift at that snow cone concession stand?" Nina asked Jenny, releasing the child.

"Yes, indeed. Because of this heat, we had steady business. We made a bundle of money on my shift. Chloe was a big help, too. Whenever anyone wanted to know the flavors we had, we just pointed at her shirt." Jenny laughed, holding Chloe still so that Nina could see the purple, orange, and green stains embedded in the shirt. "I'm on my way to the rest room now to change her, so we can have some fun. I'm glad I brought a change of clothes for both of us."

Nina laughed. She was glad that Jenny and Chloe were having fun. They deserved it. Jenny's marriage had become rather shaky in the last few months. Her husband, Earl, could be crude and insensitive, Nina knew.

"There's grape and orange and lime. All of them are good, Aunt Nina," Chloe said, pushing out her chest as though she were wearing medals.

"I bet they are, angel." She squeezed Chloe's chin. "I was supposed to work the hot dog stand, but I had an emergency delivery at the hospital that kept me from coming earlier."

"You shouldn't be worried about working. You've done enough by organizing all of this. You should just enjoy the fruits of your labor," Jenny said, lifting her wraparound sunglasses off her eyes to wipe away the sweat. "It's really great." She draped her arm around Nina's shoulder as they watched the people going here and there.

"Jenny, how are things with you and Earl?" Nina asked, lowering her voice. She worried about Jenny. Her husband had not been able to hold down a decent job. Jenny had become secretive. She was often moody with Nina whenever she tried to cheer her or get her to open up. Nina had sometimes seen bruises on her arms and face that Jenny had explained away as clumsiness. And Nina had seen Earl hanging out in the part of town where the druggies handled their business. Nina suspected that he was dabbling in drugs.

"Uh . . . okay." Jenny looked away from Nina. "I forgot to tell you, I've taken a job at that new twenty-four-hour Wal-Mart on the highway. I'm going to be working from nine to three o'clock days."

"That's all right. But I'm sure going to miss you at the clinic."

"I'm going to miss going there, too. I liked doing the volunteer work. At the moment, things are kind of tight financially for us. After I pay off a few bills, I hope to give a few hours a week when I can." She smiled nervously.

"C'mon, Mommy. You promised to buy me some balloons. You said I could ride the pony, too." Chloe tugged on her mother's hand.

"I'll be talking to you, Nina," Jenny called out as she and Chloe turned away.

"Sure. Have fun, you guys." Nina watched Jenny and Chloe walk away. She frowned. There was something going on with Jenny that she wasn't talking about. Jenny hadn't been herself lately. Several times at the clinic while Jenny worked in the reception area, Nina had caught her staring into space with her brow furrowed. Some afternoons she had arrived at work with red-rimmed eyes. Jenny attributed her condition to allergies. Nina believed the allergy was named Earl.

Nina's thoughts turned abruptly from Jenny when she came upon an art display. Her interest was piqued by a framed painting, "The Birthday Girl." It had to be hers. The eye-catching colors and the characters touched a special place in her heart. It was as though someone had stolen a slice of her life and captured it on canvas. The painting by the talented black artist was ideal for the house she had just moved into and renovated. The love-filled, mahogany faces of the mother and father, smiling proudly down at the little girl, reminded her of her deceased parents, Brenda and Lester Sterling.

Bangs framed the girl's brown face, and two big braids tied with bright pink ribbons rested behind her ears. The child wore a frilly pink dress, and she clasped her hands as though she were about to pray. Excitement lit up her eyes; her lips were puckered to blow out the candles on a cake set before her.

Studying the picture, Nina felt a twinge of sadness in her heart. That could have been her, more than twenty-some years ago.

"Kinda corny, isn't it?"

Nina looked over her shoulder to meet the gaze of Addison Wagner. Hovering over her at his six-feet-plus height, he rubbed his chin as he assessed the painting she had fallen in love with.

She smiled tentatively at him. "I don't think it's corny. I adore it. I have to have this," she said, handing it to the vendor along with several crisp bills. "How long have you been here, Addison?"

His unexpected appearance was a pleasant surprise. She was anxious to hear his opinion of the fabulous turnout for the festival. She wanted to see if he was man enough to swallow his pride and admit he had been wrong. She wanted to hear him say how marvelous she was to have come up with such a great idea.

Staring at him, Nina felt a surge of delicious warmth mingled with a sense of victory. His caramel complexion had a healthy glow, and when he smiled, his velvet-brown eyes appeared to sparkle. He looked sexy in baggy blue basketball-style shorts and a grey, perspiration-stained t-shirt.

He chuckled softly. "I was just part of the walkathon that you assigned me to at the last minute. I also helped pass out the t-shirts you ordered for all of those who withstood this Harper Falls humidity for the cause."

"Wonderful. I knew I could count on you to keep things going," she said with enthusiasm. "Let me buy you a cold drink and something to eat. How about a hot dog? The least I can do is to feed the help, since I was unable to work my shift." She accepted her wrapped painting and her change from the vendor.

"That's a deal I can't refuse. It's not every day I can get a smile like that from you—and a free meal." Addison eased the painting from Nina and slipped it beneath his arm to carry it for her. "Hey, something is different about you." He eyed her with half a grin. "Where are your glasses?"

When his arm brushed against hers ever so lightly, she felt tiny sparks of excitement. She could barely answer. "Contacts," she said matter-of-factly. She smiled, pleased that he had noticed the difference in her appearance.

"Hmm . . . they're a nice change," he said.

As they strolled to the nearest concession stand, a statuesque beauty dressed in a mini-floral sundress approached Addison. She sashayed up to him and planted a kiss on his face, leaving an imprint of lipstick.

Nina continued walking so that he wouldn't feel obliged to introduce her. She wasn't in the mood to meet any more of his too-eager women, thinking of that Mia person she'd met a few weeks ago. She hated the fact that the woman had interrupted her cozy moment with Addison. It would have been nice to share the day with him, since they had both put so much time and effort into planning it.

She noticed that Addison's handsome face had brightened at the pushy hussy. How many women did this man need to feed his ego? she wondered. She tapped her foot impatiently, waiting for the moment when he would remember she was there. The poor creature he was talking with probably had no idea that she was only one of many vying for his attention. Nina was well aware of his reputation for being a ladies' man. She had heard the rumors of his torrid romances and tumultuous relationships. Every eligible woman, and even some dissatisfied married women, wanted to snag him as her own. He was considered quite a catch with his good looks, his successful career as a physician, and his acquired wealth from his prestigious family.

Standing in line at the concession stand, Nina glanced over her shoulder toward Addison. He and the woman held hands while they chatted. She thought about disappearing in the crowd and forgetting about him. Then the woman kissed him again and waved to him as she left to catch up with some friends. Seeing Addison jogging toward her, Nina ordered a couple of hot dogs and two large lemonades.

"I didn't mean to keep you waiting. She used to work in the lab at the hospital," Addison explained.

"No problem," Nina said, accepting his explanation even though she considered his behavior rude. "Let's get out of this sun and heat for a while."

She and Addison decided to eat inside the nearby blue-and-white canvas tent to get relief from the sun. Not only was it cooler, but it held a live band that entertained other festival patrons who were relaxing.

"It feels good to be out of the heat." Addison took a long drink of his lemonade. Then he placed the cool cup to his temple, closing his eyes briefly.

"It sure does. I'm glad I had the foresight to arrange such areas," Nina said, staring around at the knots of friendly faces scattered here and there. Then she brought her gaze back to match Addison's pleasant expression. "Our community turned out better than I expected. I love it." Her face glowed with delight.

"Okay, I was wrong for doubting you. I know you've been waiting to hear me admit it." He lavished a devastating grin on her. "Your idea was right on time, so I suppose you're quite pleased with proving me wrong. It's a great day, lady."

Her defenses began to subside with his sincere praise, and her body vibrated with new life. "Thank you for the compliment, and for your help. It was work, wasn't it?" She shook her head and moaned softly, thinking over the heated debates with Addison and the six other members of the committee. "Despite all the problems we encountered, it was worth all the long hours and frustration we put into it."

"That was when I learned how stubborn you were. You showed me just how tough you can be. You kept me on my toes. Toward the end of the planning, the last thing I wanted was to get on your bad side."

She laughed softly. "I wasn't that bad, was I?" she asked as casually as she could manage. "I was just determined that we were going to pull this thing off as near perfect as possible."

"Well, you've done it." Addison grinned at her while he finished off the last of his hot dog. "Listen, there's supposed to be a great jazz ensemble performing later, when it gets dark. They're my personal favorite. How about hanging out with me for that?"

"I . . . I don't know," she said reluctantly. She didn't want to appear too excited over his invitation. "There's so many things I need to check on before the night is over."

"You need to relax, too. I'll help you make the rounds after we check out the jazz group," he vowed.

"In that case, I can't refuse." She smiled. Today would be a more-than-memorable day with her and Addison checking out the concert together.

Somewhere off in the distance outside the tent, the sounds of a group singing Motown oldies could be heard. The song, crooned by some imitators of the Four Tops, was "I Can't Help Myself."

Nina shifted her shoulders in time to the beat as though she were shaking off all the tension she had endured because of the festival and dealing with Addison and her hidden emotions.

Giving her a smile that held a deeper sense of respect, Addison bobbed his head in time with the sounds Nina was bopping with. "Come on," he suggested. "Let's get out of here and go check out that group." He rose and held out his hand to her.

She liked the warm, relaxed look on his face. As a very busy doctor at a city hospital and with a growing private practice, she hardly had the time to let it all hang out. Bursting with exhilaration from the festival as well as Addison's company, she accepted his hand and they headed in the direction of the hip-swinging music. Today she wasn't that somber professional. Today she wanted to be a young woman in search of fun.

Both of them loved the band and all the old songs they played. They sang and clapped in time to the music and laughed, amazing each other by how many of the classic songs they knew. When a younger group of musicians took the stage, singing songs that the teens related to enthusiastically, Addison went off to buy bottled water.

Standing alone and enjoying the fancy dance steps of the group, Nina was distracted when she heard her name being called above the noise. Suddenly she saw two little forms wiggling their way through the crowd to get to her. She recognized Kyra and Jamal, the eight- and nine-year-old children of her best friends, Kimberly and Doug Griffith.

"Once the kids heard that music, I couldn't hold them back," Kimberly said, lifting her sunglasses off her eyes. She greeted Nina with a hug, the way she always did when she saw her friend.

Doug smiled broadly at Nina. "The children have been bugging us all day about coming here. I didn't have a moment's peace until Kim and I gave in to bring them." He glanced around. "Some turnout. I admit I didn't expect this kind of response. And to think Addison didn't think there was going to be much to it."

"But the event is spectacular for its first time," Nina said, squeezing Doug on his elbow. "And he had to admit to me how wrong he was for mistrusting my judgment."

"I know you didn't come out here alone," Kimberly said, sliding her arm around Nina's waist. "I hope your date is somewhere in this crowd. There must be a man around. You're not wearing your glasses," her friend teased, studying Nina's face. "Hey, kid, you should have gotten rid of those things a long time ago. You've been hiding your nice features behind them for far too long."

"Thanks for the compliment. But I haven't given up my glasses completely yet. And for your information, I didn't come with a date. I came alone. You know I'm not one of those women who has to bring a date to everything. If I did, I would never go anywhere."

Nina had often felt self-conscious over being dateless. But the older she became, the less it mattered. She realized that there was a shortage of good black men because of the social problems in the country. She'd resigned herself to living her life alone. She refused to compromise her standards like Jenny, who had to have a man in her life even though he was a worthless son of a gun.

Kimberly shook her head sympathetically. "What am I going to do with you?"

"Stay out of my business." Nina chuckled softly, leaning on Kimberly's shoulder. More than once she had been the reluctant victim of Kimberly and her determined efforts to match her up with a suitable lifetime mate.

"I introduced you to two good men. You're too choosy."

"I don't think so. One of those guys was a somber mortician, and the other one was . . . well, I guess it's best not to say anything about him, other than that it was a waste of my good time dating him even that once."

"So you didn't like them. Give me another chance, and I'm sure to find the right one for you. Girlfriend, you need more than work in your life. You can pretend all you want. But there comes a time in every woman's life when she wants a sweet man to warm her bed and to fill her life with some love and laughter."

"Ease up, Kimberly. This is not the time for you to lecture me on my biological clock and my needs. Come and enjoy the music." Today was not the day for this worn-out bit of girlfriend conversation, Nina thought.

Soon the beat of the Kool and the Gang tune, "Celebrate," had the crowd rocking. Kyra and Jamal, who loved to dance, tugged on Nina to join them.

She fell into step with their jaunty rhythm. Kyra and Jamal giggled at the extra steps Nina added as she got her groove on. She sang along with the song. She felt the music in her blood, and it made her heart feel happy. She snatched Jamal's White

Sox cap off his head and jammed it on her head, turning it backwards. Her hard-stepping moves made her pecan complexion dewy with perspiration. Her brown eyes glinted with humor, and she winked at the kids who were delighted that she could keep up with them.

"C'mon, Uncle Addison, you can dance with Aunt Nina," Kyra shouted at Addison as he reappeared with two bottles of water dangling on his fingertips.

"Oh no, not me," Addison exclaimed. He smiled awkwardly at Nina. "Frankly, I don't want to look like a fool. I'm good at most things, but dancing is not one of them."

She shrugged her shoulders without breaking her rhythm.

"C'mon, guys, keep up with me," Nina urged the children. She could feel Addison studying the way she moved. Stealing a glance at him, she could tell by the way he beamed at her that he liked what he saw. She liked the way he looked at her; it made her feel sexy. She directed a smile at him as he clapped his hands and swayed to the music.

Gazing into his piercing, mischievous brown eyes, Nina felt her heart race. What was happening to her? She had tried so hard not to live in the past and the memories of those days when she had a crush on Addison. If she had a dollar for the number of times she had fantasized about being with him, she would probably be a millionaire, she mused. But that was so long ago, when she had been a lonely, shy, wretched high school kid. The emotions she still might harbor could be detrimental. She didn't want to be one of the many women whom he toyed with. Her emotions were too precious to be trivialized.

When the song ended, Addison handed her a bottle of water. "You've missed your calling. If you get tired of delivering babies, I'm sure you can find work as a dancer in those soul music videos like they play on MTV," he teased. "Right, kids?" he asked, turning to Kyra and Jamal for support.

35

Kyra's and Jamal's faces beamed at Nina with admiration that she could be such a performer.

"Quit it, Addison," Nina said, smiling. She took a long sip of water to cool off and turned her back to him to talk with Kimberly.

Doug sidled up to Addison and the two fell into a conversation regarding an upcoming golf date.

"So, you came alone, huh?" Kimberly grinned like a Cheshire cat. "You two look mighty chummy to me. He is perfect. Really, he is. I'd thought about pairing you two guys, but I didn't think it would work. I mean, you two see quite a bit of each other at the hospital and the free clinic, and I figured there just weren't any sparks, and . . ."

"Slow down, Kim. Addison and I didn't come together. He and I ran into each other, and we were just passing time together. That's all. Nothing more."

Kimberly gave Nina a knowing look. "Sure. Okay."

"Stop looking at me that way. I tell you, there's nothing for you to put your nose into."

"I don't know about that. I saw the way the man was looking at you. He thinks of you as more than a friend. Believe me on this one." Kimberly nudged Nina and winked. "If you'd seen that romantic stare he laid on you, it would have made you weak."

"Will you quit that? You're getting on my nerves. I'm not Addison's type. And you know that." She thought of the two sexy, attractive women she'd seen him with. Those women had flirting down to an art. The only way Nina knew how to challenge a man was with her mind, her intellect.

"You're afraid of being his type," Kimberly said. "You are a good looking woman, Nina. You hide yourself in the kind of clothes you wear. You refuse to wear make-up. Most of the time, you walk around looking like a mousy school girl. Thank goodness you finally decided to get rid of those ugly glasses!"

"I don't have time to primp and dress to please a man. I dress for comfort. I dress to please myself. And I'm discovering that contacts are easier than glasses. That's all!" She shifted her shoulders confidently. She depicted an ease she didn't really feel.

Kimberly let out a skeptical snort.

"And I'm not afraid of Addison either," Nina went on. "In the last few weeks we've been quite cordial with each other. There might be a chance for a simple friendship. He and I are even going to hang out at the jazz concert here tonight."

"You rascal, you!" exclaimed Kimberly. "It sounds as though there might be hope for you yet." She rested her arm around Nina's shoulder and turned her toward Addison's direction. "Make the most of the evening," Kimberly instructed. "Just look at that gorgeous man. I'm a married woman, and when I look at him, I wonder what kind of lover he is. Of course, my Doug is quite fine for me. But I'm human. I don't pretend, as I know you do, that no man moves me in the special way God meant."

"Okay. He is . . . I do think he is rather fine and sexy," Nina admitted. "Satisfied? And shame on you for lusting over another man."

"Be quiet, girlfriend. Just because I'm married doesn't mean I'm dead. Men check out pretty women all the time, so why can't women do the same?" Kimberly said, eyeing her friend with amusement. "You know Doug means the world to me. And anyway, you just try to turn this evening thing with Addison into something much more. You understand?"

Nina anchored her feet and placed a hand on her hip. "What do you want from me, woman? I'll be with him for one evening."

"I'm determined to put some romance in your life. I want you to know the kind of happiness I've had in my marriage."

Standing not too far from Nina, Addison could not peel his eyes away from her. Though Doug was babbling about his golf game, he had tuned him out. The sight of her dancing and having fun with the kids had made him think of Nina as more than the cool professional woman that she prided herself on being.

Whenever he saw her at the hospital or clinic, her figure was hidden in hospital scrubs or long skirts and loose-fitting blouses. Her reddish-brown, long hair was pulled away from her face in a ponytail, and until today, huge-framed eyeglasses masked the sparkle he had seen in her eyes. His eyes caressed her form in the flattering, floral-print shorts set. Her body was fine. Her breasts were full, and her hips small yet rounded to perfection. Her shapely legs and firm thighs made his pulse race with sexual fantasies of holding her captive beneath him.

Doug brought Addison out of his stimulating thoughts by slapping him hard on the back. "You aren't listening to me, knucklehead. You're too busy checking out Nina. I know that look of yours, man. You ought to be ashamed of yourself for undressing that woman," Doug teased.

"Man, leave me alone." He shrugged Doug's hand off his shoulder. "Has she always been this fine? Or have I just been a blind fool?"

"Do I hear the sounds of the great lover being reeled in, my man?" Doug laughed.

"You're too much, man." Addison smiled mischievously. "But it could be interesting getting caught by her. Yes, it could."

Nina must have felt him watching her. She glanced over at Addison and smiled. He matched hers with an even broader smile.

The tender look she lavished on him was nearly as good as a kiss. Addison could feel his temperature rising a couple of notches. He took a long drink from his bottle of water.

"Nina is a good woman, but I can't picture you with her," Doug said. "She's kind of innocent when it comes to men and relationships. Nor does she fit the profile of the kind of woman you like to romp with. I'm used to seeing you with those sexy, bronze beauties with luscious curves and bodies made for loving."

Addison's gaze fixed on Nina as she began to dance some more with the kids. In that moment, the sexy, bronze beauties couldn't hold a candle to what he saw or what he was beginning to feel for Nina Sterling. It would be interesting to see what she was like in bed, just once. But he wouldn't dare consider a relationship with her.

For both their sakes, it was best that he not pursue Nina Sterling—no matter how much she turned him on. He used to believe in romance and love, until Vanessa. Since his involvement with her had ended bitterly, he hadn't been fit for a decent woman like Nina. After being disillusioned by love once, he decided not to risk his heart again.

Chapter III

"Sue, make sure this patient returns in a week," Nina said to the nurse who worked at the free clinic. "Her blood pressure needs to be monitored. Review the low-salt diet with her again. Please stress its importance in her condition."

As Nina handed the patient's chart to Sue Kerry, she glanced at the back door. It burst open abruptly.

Chloe appeared and leaned against the door to hold it open with her weight. Her mother, Jenny, skulked through like a kicked dog. She was bent at the waist, holding her side. There were dark bruises on her freckled light complexion, and her lip was cut and bleeding. The white shorts she wore were dirty, and her t-shirt was stained with blood and dirt. One sleeve was ripped and hung in ragged shreds.

"Sue, come on! Help me," Nina cried. She rushed to meet Jenny as she limped up the hall. "It's okay, Jenny. We'll take care of you." Nina seethed with anger over the pitiful sight before her. She didn't need an explanation for the woman's condition.

What would it take for her friend to see that that man didn't have it in him to change?

As Nina and Sue moved to support Jenny between them, she burst into tears. Chloe, already upset, also began to cry.

"Sue, take Chloe into the playroom. I'll help Jenny into exam room two. Then get Addison in here," Nina said. Trauma patients were his specialty, and she wanted the best for Jenny. She turned to Chloe, who didn't want to leave her mother. "She's going to be all right, sweetheart. Go on with Sue so I can help your mama."

Sue Kerry seized the child's hand and led her in the opposite direction. She attempted to distract her by telling her about the new puzzles they'd received.

"You've got to get away from that man," Nina said through clenched teeth. She guided Jenny onto the exam table. "My God, what caused him to treat you this way?" She gently stripped off Jenny's clothes and helped her into a gown.

Wincing with pain, Jenny eased herself onto the table, unwilling to answer. She trembled and sobbed as though her heart were breaking.

"What do we have here?" Addison asked, hurrying into the exam room.

Nina stepped away from Jenny in order for Addison to examine her.

At the sight of the battered woman, his eyes dimmed and the corners of his mouth twitched. He lifted Jenny's hospital gown to inspect the major source of her pain. When he touched the bruised areas on her side, she flinched. Her breath was short, and she complained of dizziness. He called in another nurse and directed her to take Jenny down the hall for X-rays to validate his diagnosis of broken ribs and a punctured lung.

The nurse, with the assistance of Addison and Nina,

transferred Jenny onto a gurney. Then the nurse carted the woman out of the examination room.

While Jenny was being X-rayed, Addison questioned Nina. "Who did this to her?" he demanded. "Lover? Husband? Monster?"

"Her husband, Earl Martin."

"The man must be a mental case. He should be locked up. But of course she won't hear of it, will she? That's usually the scenario," he said impatiently. "I've witnessed cases like this all too often." His voice sounded weary, and his face lacked its usual warmth. "I just can't grasp how any man can do this to a woman he is supposed to love. Nor can I get used to seeing this kind of brutality against any woman or children. I'll never understand it." His brow furrowed with concern. He rubbed his temples and closed his eyes. "We'll probably have to admit her to the hospital. I suspect she is seriously injured. I'm going to check on her." He marched away from Nina toward the X-ray room.

"What did he say?" Jenny asked Nina once she was settled back in the examining room.

"He'll talk to you in a bit. He's waiting on the results of the X-ray." Nina took her friend's hand. "You have no business with Earl, Jenny," Nina said.

"He . . . he has been under a lot of strain," Jenny said. "He's been trying to get work to handle all our bills, but he hasn't been able to find any."

"Pshaw! He's not serious about finding work. He's high most of the time. I see him hanging out in that crime pit downtown where people buy drugs."

Addison returned to the room, looking somber. "Young lady, we're going to have to admit you to the hospital. The X-ray shows several broken ribs and a punctured lung. If we don't get you to the hospital soon, your lungs could fill with fluid. Your condition is very serious."

Jenny scowled. "I don't have time to lay up in no hospital. I have my new job at Wal-Mart, and I have no one to care for Chloe."

"You don't have a choice in this one if you want to live," Addison said.

"Stop being silly, Jenny," Nina said. "I'm speaking as a friend, not as a doctor. You need medical attention. You have no choice but to go to the hospital."

"I'm going to call the hospital to make arrangements. I'm also going to call the paramedics to transport you," Addison said, heading for the door. "And I won't listen to any excuses." In a moment, he was gone.

Jenny's face turned to a mask of terror. "Stop him, Nina! I'm telling you. I can't go. Earl can't take care of Chloe. He does all right with her for the few hours I'm at work, but you're talking about days here." She placed her hand on her forehead, frowned, and groaned. "Phew! The room is spinning."

"Relax. You'll be better once you get to the hospital."

"No hospital! I can't leave my baby with him. He's . . . he's not that responsible." Jenny shifted restlessly on the examining table, grimacing with pain. "It seems the older Chloe gets, the more she looks like her real father, Willie."

"And? I never knew that made any difference to Earl."

Jenny inhaled and exhaled as if she were trying to find enough breath to speak. "Nina, he accuses me of holding back my affection from him. He reminds me of how I used to look at Willie and how I used to smile for Willie. He tells me how he used to envy Willie for having me as his girl." Jenny's voice was husky from pain.

"Is this the reason he pounds on you when he gets the urge? He feels as though he's competing with a ghost?"

"I don't know. I've tried my best to convince him he is my man—the only man I care about." She closed her eyes and

43

pursed her lips. "He . . . he's jealous of Chloe. He accuses me of giving her more attention."

"But she's your child. She should be your main priority." Nina shook her head. "He needs to get off those drugs, and you need to get away from him until he gets straight."

"He's tried. I've been trying to stand by him until he can get sober." Jenny's speech was measured, as though each word hurt. "Nina, you don't understand what it's like to need a man. Earl can be the sweetest man in the world when he's clean. I promised to stick it out with him. He needs me."

Listening to her go on about her so-called love, Nina stared at her impatiently.

"Don't judge me," Jenny snapped. "If you had a love life, you'd know and understand what I'm talking about."

"Enough of this. My life is not in question or in jeopardy," Nina said curtly. "Anyway, this isn't the time or the place. The most important thing right now is to get you transferred to the hospital, where you can get the proper care you need."

"You've got to take Chloe for me."

"What?" Her suggestion made Nina feel ill at ease. She didn't want any part of Jenny's domestic problems.

"You've got to take Chloe." Jenny's frightened eyes locked into hers.

Nina wouldn't hold her gaze. She refused to let Jenny run a guilt trip on her. "I want to help you, Jenny—I really do. But that's something I can't do. I don't have the time, nor do I have any idea of how to care for her."

"Earl will neglect her." Jenny tried to raise herself up, but she was too weak. Her face twisted with her discomfort. "Ouch," she groaned. She closed her teary eyes briefly, then opened them. "He beats my baby too often for next to nothing. He gets carried away with it. He . . . he's left bruises . . ." Jenny couldn't look at Nina. "She's just a child who can be too playful

44

at times. And she knocks over things, like any child does who is active." Jenny's breathing was labored. "That bugs him, especially if he's coming down from his drugs. He does it to hurt me, I know." Her voice trembled. "Now, can't you see why I don't want to leave her alone with him?"

There was so much Nina wanted to say, but she forced herself to keep quiet. Despite it all, she knew Jenny loved that sorry man. Jenny had a history of falling in love with all the wrong kinds of men. Willie, Chloe's father, hadn't been much better. He had made his living from selling stolen property. Yet Jenny had loved him until his death. Nina knew that she, of all people, had no right to judge Jenny. If she had not been dedicated to the dream her mother had embedded in her, she could very well have ended up like Jenny, who managed to make the worst choices in men. Jenny was the kind of woman who thrived on having a man around. Unfortunately, it was the way she validated her self-worth.

"Nina, you're the only person I would trust Chloe to. I don't have anyone else to turn to while I have to be laid up in the hospital," Jenny implored, tears welling in her eyes. "Say you'll do it. Please."

Nina stared at her, trying to come up with a tactful excuse. "I don't have time to babysit. When I'm not here at the clinic, I have a private practice to maintain," she explained. "I'm called out at all hours of the night to be with my patients. Can't you understand how inconvenient it would be for me to have a child around?"

Devastated, Jenny covered her eyes with the heels of her hands and sobbed.

Hovering over her friend, Nina lifted Jenny's trembling hands from her face and held them to comfort her. "Chloe will be fine," she said, feeling emotions well up in her throat from the sadness she saw in Jenny's eyes. She was beginning to feel guilty for not accepting the responsibility Jenny wanted to lay on her. "Chloe will be well taken care of. I'll call . . . call social services. They'll place her in a good home for the few days you have to be separated from her. I'll be glad to check on her. That's the best I can do."

Snatching her hands out of Nina's, Jenny's expression turned sullen. "Don't bring those social workers into my business. You must be trying to get my baby taken away from me." She glared at Nina. "What can you be thinking, woman? You and I both have some awful memories of the system."

Nina felt helpless. "It's the best I can come up with. Certainly things are better now than when you and I were in foster care. And I told you I would keep tabs on her."

"Forget it." Jenny struggled to sit up on the hard table. Her face twisted with pain, and she broke out in a sweat. "Give me a shot or some pills to ease my pain so I can get out of here and take my child home. I'll be all right. I'll be just fine." Her voice was low and strained, revealing her disappointment in Nina.

Taking her by the shoulders, Nina tried to ease Jenny back down on the table. "You can't leave. You need medical attention that you can only get in a hospital."

Despite her misery, Jenny shoved Nina away. "Leave me alone," she muttered. "Stop acting like you care. I thought I could count on you, even though you've become a big-time doctor. I see you've forgotten where you come from, and how it is for folks like me." Her eyes glazed, shutting Nina out of her world.

Nina sighed heavily and gripped the stethoscope around her neck. She hated it when people she had known or grown up with in Harper Falls threw comments like that at her. No one seemed to remember how hard she had worked and struggled to get to college and then through medical school. Her life had been no bed of roses. There had been many times when no one wanted to be bothered with her. However, she tried not to dwell on the past and all the horrible memories of life in foster care. Had she done that, she never would have been able to move forward and accomplish the things she had.

Because she had become a physician—a black physician— she was expected to right all the wrongs in the lives of everyone from her community. Everyone wanted her to be a role model—the trophy for all other deprived blacks. Certainly she did not mind helping or doing what she could to give back to the black community of Harper Falls. Hadn't she been the one to push to have the free clinic opened near the Banbury Park Projects? Hadn't she set up and supervised a special program with St. Luke's Hospital to have black high school students from the neighborhood work as volunteers, so that they could learn about medical careers? Still, it never seemed to be enough. There was always someone to tell her she could do more. How much more was expected of her? she thought, trying to suppress her ire.

"Don't start that bull, Jenny," she said. "It's not fair. Where I came from has made me what and who I am today."

Addison suddenly entered the room. "The paramedics are here to transport Jenny," he announced in a professional tone.

"I ain't going. I can't go," Jenny protested vehemently.

Addison swung his gaze to Nina, searching for an explanation to his patient's irrationality. After all, she'd given consent for him to care for Jenny.

"I'm not going to no hospital. I've got my kid to look out for, and that's that." Jenny gripped the sides of the examining table to show that she wouldn't be moved. "Give me something for

47

the pain. Tape up my sides or something, then let me go, so I can go home and handle my business."

"You're not making sense," Addison said, frowning. "Your condition can worsen and become critical." He stared down at the thin woman; she refused to look at him. "We're going to get you to hospital where you'll get the care you need." He patted her arm. "Don't worry about your child. We can make arrangements for her. Social services will be out for her and see to it that she's taken care of properly." He moved away from Jenny to open the door and motioned to the waiting paramedics. "Fellows, come on in. The patient is ready to be transported."

"No, I can't go!" Jenny cried in a loud voice.

The paramedics entered the room, pushing a gurney. They rolled it next to where Jenny lay.

"Nina, please. Don't let them take my baby. You take her. Help me this once. Please," Jenny implored.

Addison's piercing eyes studied Nina's face. "What's going on?" he asked.

"She . . . she wants me to take Chloe," Nina explained. "She doesn't trust the girl's stepfather to take care of her. She wants me to be Chloe's guardian until she is better."

"That's out of the question, and you know it," Addison snapped impatiently, scribbling on Jenny's chart. "Have Sue call social services to come get her child. They'll take care of her."

Chloe came running into the examination room to her mother. Sue Kerry followed close behind her. "Mommy, I heard you fussing. What's wrong, Mommy?" Chloe leaned against the table. Jenny touched the side of her face and lavished a loving look upon her only child. Chloe's eyes flew frantically to the doctors, then to the paramedics with the gurney.

48

Nina couldn't bear the alarm or the tears she saw in Chloe's eyes. She knelt to be eye level with her and took the little girl's hands in hers. "Listen to me, baby. Your mother is very sick. We're sending her to the hospital to stay for a couple of days to get better."

"We're going to the hospital?" Chloe responded, placing a finger in the corner of her mouth and tugging nervously. She looked in her mother's direction, sending her a worried look.

"You . . . you can't go," said Nina. "Only your mama." She smiled to ease the child's tension as the paramedics helped Jenny onto the gurney.

Chloe snatched her hands out of Nina's. "Don't take her. She might die there!" she whined. She dashed to her mother's side.

Nina rushed to Chloe and pulled the grief-stricken child away. The scene tugged at her heart. Tears pooled in her eyes. She remembered the last time she'd seen her own mother in the hospital, and her heart swelled with sadness. Her widowed mother had suffered a heart attack. Nina had been twelve years old at the time. Vividly, she remembered the ride to the hospital in the emergency van, the sound of her mother's labored breathing, and the way she had lain nearly lifeless on the stretcher. She remembered holding her mother's hand and squeezing it to will her to get better. She remembered her mother uttering "I love you" before she took her last breath. She remembered falling on her mother and sobbing and shaking her, hoping to bring her back to life. She could never put Chloe through that!

"Calm down, Chloe," she said. She slipped her arm around the child's waist to control her and steered her away from her ailing mother. "Your mother is going to be just fine. You don't have to be afraid." She turned the child to face her and knelt before her, staring into her tear-glistening eyes. "Everything will be fine." Nina glanced across the room to meet Jenny's pleading eyes. How could she deny Jenny's request under these circumstances? She smiled reassuringly at Chloe. "How would you like to stay at my place until your mother gets better?"

Jenny peered at Nina with a smile of relief that lit her bruised face. "Thank God. Thank you." Jenny sighed, placing her hand over her heart.

Addison grunted, shook his head, and pursed his lips in disgust as he signed some forms and handed them to the paramedics.

Jenny wiggled her finger at Chloe to come to her. "Angel, give me a hug and a kiss. Be a good girl for me, okay? We'll be together soon."

"Please move you arms to your sides, ma'am," instructed one paramedic. "It's time to leave."

"I'll be right behind you guys," Addison called after the men as they disappeared out of the room with Jenny. "I want to be there when my patient is prepped for intensive care."

Chloe returned to Nina. She sobbed as she leaned against Nina's leg.

"Everything is going to be all right, baby." Nina lifted Chloe off the floor and comforted her with a reassuring hug and a smile.

"Sue, will you look out for Chloe for a few minutes?" Addison asked the nurse.

"Certainly, doctor." Sue took a reluctant Chloe from Nina.

Addison shoved one hand in his pocket and jammed the other one angrily on his hip. "Have you lost your mind?" he asked, scowling. "We're supposed to call social services, and you know it. You're a professional. You can't allow yourself to become emotionally involved," he rebuked. "You don't get tangled up in these patients' lives. Ever! You're risking too much.

If something happens to that child while she's under your care, your whole career could be on the line."

Nina held back her angry retort and marched toward the door. Why did he have to lecture her? He isn't my superior, she thought. "I don't have to listen to you. I'm ready to assume responsibility for my actions. That child needs me. Jenny needs me. She is more than a patient to me, so just mind your own business," she fumed. She straightened her shoulders and stalked out of the room.

Away from Addison and around the corner from the examining room, Nina leaned against the wall. The cool feel of the tile eased the tension within her. Addison had a way of making her second-guess herself. He had been practicing only a few years longer than she, and yet he always had a way of making her feel inferior to him. She might not be the best doctor in the world, but she was a good doctor—one who worked hard to learn how to give her patients the best care. She didn't just see her patients as a clump of symptoms.

He came around the corner, carrying his small black bag and a folder. Spotting Nina, he paused. "I'm sorry for what I said back there. I was out of line. You were right. I have no business telling you what to do in your personal life." He tucked Jenny's folder under his arm. "Well, I'm on my way to the hospital to check on Jenny. You shouldn't have any more serious problems with the patients who are left." He hustled halfway down the hall and stopped. He looked over his shoulder at Nina and smiled warmly. "If you need any help, let me know." Then he continued down the hallway and out the door.

Nina exhaled a long sigh of contentment after Addison's apology. He was not the kind of man who typically apologized for his haughtiness in medical matters. She moved toward the snack room to check on Chloe before she finished seeing the rest of the day's patients. Seeing a gloomy-looking Chloe sitting at a table across from Sue and munching on a cookie, Nina felt burdened by the commitment she had made to Jenny.

Addison is right, she thought. I have no business taking on the responsibilities of this child. What could I have been thinking?

"Dr. Sterling. Carrie, in exam room one. Her water has broken," another nurse announced, breaking Nina's reverie.

She took a deep breath. What a day! she thought, hustling to check on her seventeen-year-old maternity patient who was going to be a mother for the second time.

Chapter IV

After Addison had seen to it that Jenny was situated in the intensive care unit and had checked on a few of his other patients, his thoughts returned to Nina. Checking his watch, he noticed that it was nearly nine o'clock. He wondered how she was making out with Chloe this first evening as her guardian. He remembered how comforting and patient she had been with the weepy child as she watched her mother being shuttled off to the hospital. A glow, a lovely aura, came off Nina, touching his heart and stirring up emotions that he didn't want to feel for any woman. It had been more than a week since that festival he and Nina had organized. And he still had the memorable images of her softer side in his mind. He'd pushed them impatiently from his thoughts. He wanted the kind of women who liked a good time, casual sex with no strings attached.

Glancing out into the night from the picture window in the doctor's lounge, he observed flashes of lightning. Heavy rain began to douse the windows at a steady pace. He reached into his pocket and unfolded his cellular phone to dial Nina's home number. He just wanted to make sure they were okay. That was all. She certainly wasn't any more to him than a friend and colleague.

A heavy downpour of rain fell at nine-fifteen as Nina pulled into the driveway of her house on Marple Drive. Thunder grumbled, and flashes of lightning brighten the night. Looking at a worn, sleeping Chloe slumped over in her seat with the seat belt harnessing her, Nina sighed. She was as weary as Chloe. She'd spent hours with social services, arranging to become the girl's guardian. Then she had taken the sweet child shopping. There hadn't been much time to eat, with all the details she had to attend to. Nina had fed the little girl potato chips and soda to quell her hunger until they could get to her house. Going to Jenny's place to retrieve clothing for Chloe was out of the question. Nina didn't want to get into it with that man who had given Jenny nothing but misery since he had been in her life.

Raindrops hit her while she struggled to unfasten Chloe from the seat belt. She tried her best not to wake the little girl. The deep sleep was good for her after all she had been through today.

Finally freeing Chloe, she carried her limp form toward the house, with two large shopping bags dangling from her wrists. She trotted hurriedly as the rain fell faster and harder. She stepped onto the porch. A crash of lightning caused her to gasp with its unexpected boom. Chloe twitched and moaned softly. Nina shifted her in her arms so that she could unlock the door. Chloe wrapped her arms around Nina's neck, making it difficult for her to place the key in the latch while juggling the bags.

"It's okay, Chloe. I've got you. We're at my house, where you'll be safe," Nina said in a soothing voice.

After Nina had pulled off Chloe's damp clothing and the child had not awakened, she knew that she was asleep for the night. She slipped the new store-bought nightshirt onto her and tucked her into bed in the guest room. Then she tiptoed out of the room to her living room, where she collapsed onto the sofa and smoothed her rain-soaked hair. What a hectic time it had been, trying to shop with Chloe! The five-year-old had wanted to wander around in the store while Nina tried to figure out what clothing size best fit her. This was more work than she had imagined. Motherhood was definitely underrated, she mused. She had only had Chloe a few hours, and she was completely frazzled after dealing with her demands and needs.

The telephone on the other side of the room rang. Nina scowled. She hoped it wasn't a maternity patient. As yet, she had no plans for a babysitter for such emergencies. She made it to the phone on the fourth ring.

"Is she there with you?" a deep, angry voice demanded.

"Who is this?" Nina's heart raced at hearing the strange tone.

There was a moment of silence. "Her daddy, that's who. You have no business with my kid, lady. Jenny is crazy to think she can keep that girl from me. She is my child. I've done more for her than her own old man ever thought of doing. It's me she calls Daddy." His speech was slurred, as though he were drunk. "Jenny is a stupid fool. She's got no business laying up in a hospital. She ain't that sick. I can look out for her and the kid." He paused and breathed heavily into the receiver. "Listen up, I don't need no charity or some uppity female doctor all in my business. I'm coming to get her! I know where you live, lady."

Nina clutched the receiver. "You can't have her. Jenny wants me to keep her while she's in the hospital. I have papers from the legal clinic that give me the right," she informed him in a cool, no-nonsense tone. She hoped he wouldn't challenge her further. Although the child called him Daddy, Earl hadn't adopted her legally.

"What did you have to do all of that for? I'm no monster," he snapped.

He sure acted like a monster, Nina thought. If he hadn't pounded on Jenny as if she were nothing, she wouldn't lay hooked to some machine in a hospital, away from her daughter.

"Jenny thought it best for Chloe to be cared for by a woman." Nina thought this explanation would calm his anger.

"You're lying to me. I've been taking care of that girl. She's got you people thinking I'm some kind of freak. I'm not. I want that girl with me. I know what's best for her," he ranted.

"If you hadn't hurt Jenny, Chloe would be with you," Nina said irritably. She wanted the conversation to end. Talking to him was a waste of time and energy.

"You can't prove nothing. I can't help it if Jenny is a clumsy b*@*#." His voice was oddly pitched.

Nina seethed with anger, listening to this fool. "You ought to be locked up. You're not fit to be around . . ."

"You can't keep me from that girl. I'm coming for her. You'd better do the right thing, or else I might have to carve you up!"

Nina grabbed her ear as Earl slammed down the phone. Fear seeped through her. She knew she had provoked him by refusing to give in to his demands. Would he come after her for what she had said? Take back his daughter? In a sudden panic, she rushed to check the front and back doors to make certain that the locks were secured.

She went into the kitchen for a glass of water. Her mouth was as dry as cotton. She took a deep breath to ease her tension. Surely that man wasn't crazy enough to try to start trouble with her. Maybe he only meant to psych her out with fear, she assumed, the way he did with Jenny to manipulate her.

She was merely trying to assist a friend who seemed desperate for help.

Remembering the fright in Jenny's eyes and the urgency of her plea for Chloe's protection, Nina suddenly knew she was in trouble way over her head, trapped in the midst of Jenny's domestic problems. A known drug addict and alcoholic, Earl could continue to harass her verbally or even physically for disrespecting him and making him look like a punk. From Nina's observations, he wasn't the most rational man even when he was sober. And with his substance abuse problems, he had proven—by banging Jenny around—that he could be crazy.

The phone rang again. Nina jumped at the sound. Anxiety mounted within her. Staring at the phone, she willed it to stop ringing. She didn't want to argue with Earl. From the way he spoke and his angry words, she was sure he was high on something.

The phone continued to ring. Nina didn't want to answer it. However, she knew she must. It could be a call concerning Jenny, or it could be one of her patients. More than likely it was Earl, calling to continue to taunt her. Regardless, she knew she had to answer it.

A curtain of rain hit the windows; the thunder seemed to rock the house. A flash of lightning turned the night into day for a split second, which reminded Nina of a bad horror movie where the helpless heroine was always attacked by the villain. As the phone continued to ring, she stared at it, wishing it would stop. She didn't want to have to deal with Earl anymore. When the phone didn't cease ringing, she reluctantly answered it. She held the receiver pressed to her ear without uttering the usual greeting. If it was Earl, maybe this tactic would cause him to become impatient and hang up and leave her alone.

"Nina? Hello . . . hello?"

Relief surged through her. It was Addison. "It's you!"

"Thank God! I thought something had happened to you . . . What took you so long to answer?"

"It's been awful," she admitted. "Earl, Jenny's husband, called. He's threatening me. He wants Chloe. He says he knows where I live. He's drunk or high—tripping off something."

"Damn him! Now do you see what I meant when I warned you about getting involved? Make sure your doors are locked. You can't take his threats lightly. He's a mean mother. You saw how he brutalized that woman. I want you to call the police as soon as you hang up. I'm on my way to your house. I don't know how fast I can make it across town in this storm, but I'll be there as soon as I can."

Nina hung up the phone, feeling less apprehensive. Knowing Addison was coming was a welcome comfort. The lights in the house blinked twice and then went out. She cursed, standing there smothered in darkness. A power failure.

Moving to the nearest window, she peered out from her living room. Her neighbors were without lights as well. Her glance landed on a battered van parked behind her car. It had several dents on the side, and the back fender was lopsided. In fact, the whole car appeared to be leaning to one side. An imposing figure was hunched ominously over the wheel. Oh no! Was it Earl, determined to seize Chloe?

Stumbling back through the dark room to find the phone, she hit her knee on the corner of an end table. The pain immobilized her momentarily. Just then, she heard the creaking of a car door. Her heart quivered with fear. Hobbling across the room, she fumbled until she grasped the phone. She punched 911. She couldn't get a dial tone. In growing panic, she repeated her actions. Oh no! The phone line was dead! No lights—now no phone. And a madman was out to get her. Would she be able to protect herself and Chloe against this maniac? Standing in the darkness, she felt a shiver run up and down her spine. She heard heavy footfalls on the front steps. The squeaking boards made an eerie sound that gave her goosebumps. She jumped as the front doorknob rattled. She heard angry shouts. It sounded like a possessed demon, demanding to get in.

She staggered through the house to get to Chloe. Reaching the guest room, she locked the door and shoved the small vanity dresser in front of it. She climbed onto the bed and gathered the sleeping child in her arms, hugging her to comfort her and herself. She was trembling in terror. She hoped Addison would arrive soon to put a halt to this nightmare. The thunder seemed louder, the lightning harsher, the rain ceaseless. Earl kicked the door several times to gain entrance, making the wood crackle. Feeling helpless, Nina began to cry silently.

She heard pounding on the bedroom window. It rattled as though the glass would shatter at any minute. She squealed and jumped off the bed, clutching Chloe so tightly that the child woke up and started to whimper. The other window rattled more ominously than the first. Nina gasped. Her body jerked in anxious spasms. Sooner or later, the drugged lunatic would force his way in to take Jenny's child. She felt weak with helplessness.

Hearing her name being shouted above the wild noises of the storm, she crept fearfully toward the window. As a flash of lightning cut across the sky, she recognized Addison. Her heart leapt with joy. He pointed toward her front door. With a squirming Chloe cradled in her arms, she made her way back through the darkened house to admit him.

"Thank heaven!" She wanted to rush to his soaking form and embrace him.

"Are you guys okay?" he asked, entering the house. He touched her arm to comfort her.

Nina hugged Chloe. The places on her flesh where Addison's wet hand rested felt as though he had singed her. His simple, caring touch sent surges of delicious warmth through her, making her almost forget the horror she'd endured.

"A bit shaken, but fine," she said. "There was that van in my driveway. I thought it was Earl. I expected some weird antic from him."

In the darkened room, she couldn't see his face. But as he spoke, his tall, straight silhouette revealed his confidence. "They—the police—have him," he said. "He was trying to jimmy the lock when I slipped up on him. He mumbled something about having the right to see you-know-who." He reached over and patted Chloe on the head. "I called the police from my phone. I tried to call you back to let you know I was nearby, but I couldn't get through. I figured there was trouble with the line because of the storm. I beat the police here. By the time they arrived, Earl and I were exchanging blows. What a fool! I tried to talk to him, and he started swinging at me."

"Po-lice," Chloe repeated. "They come to our house all the time. They come when Daddy makes Mama cry by hurting her. They point their finger at him. They feel all over him for his medicine." Chloe touched Nina's face and rested her forehead to hers. "Is Mama outside with the police?" Chloe wiggled against Nina, trying to get down out of her arms. "Let me go to her."

"No, Chloe. Take it easy, sweetheart," Nina said, holding the child more tightly.

"Your mother is still in the hospital, getting well to be with you soon," Addison added in a soothing tone.

Listening to him, Nina smiled with admiration. He was a big-time internist and was usually indifferent to children who came to the clinic. Most of the time he only dealt with adult patients.

"The officers want to know if you want to lock this fellow up," Addison said. "You can, you know. After all, he was attempting to break in." He stood so close to her that she could feel his words traveling through her body.

She stepped back from the unnerving energy that flowed from him. At a time like this! she thought. She was grateful that the lights were out. Had he seen her face, he would have guessed the effect he was having on her.

"I only want him to leave me alone," Nina said. "I don't want any distractions while I'm trying to focus on Chloe's and my life. The next time he comes around, though, I will press charges. Tell the officers to make that clear."

"You're a better person than I," Addison said. "Look, you need to take out a restraining order on him. I have a feeling the next time he gets high, he will get bold and come around again. He isn't interested in his responsibility as a parent. This is all about control and power, and getting back at Jenny for coming to the clinic and going to the hospital. She's divulged his dirty secret. And he doesn't like it one bit."

"Exactly," she agreed. "In spite of what she's been through, she's still defending him. She still loves him. I just don't get it."

"Ah . . . the power of love. So many rational people have done so many foolish things in the name of love. Even *moi*. Oh, boy." He sighed. "Let me go and talk to the officers, so this can be settled. When I come back, I'll get a towel from you. I feel like a drowned rat."

As he stepped past her, she noticed how disheveled he was from his fight with Earl. She was surprised yet grateful that Addison of all people had gone out of his way to help and protect her.

She moved to the window to peer out onto the street. She saw the police officer follow the small-framed Earl to his van while he retrieved his keys. The two officers talked with him, then shoved him into the backseat of the police car and drove away.

In a few moments, Addison's tall frame burst through the door, allowing the coolness of the rainy night to follow him.

"Well, he's gone," Addison said. "He was drunk, so they wouldn't allow him to drive. They gave him a warning not to give you any more trouble. I'm going to call my garage and have them send a tow truck to get his van out of here. I'll even foot the bill. I don't want him to have a reason to show up and bother you."

"Thanks." Her voice revealed her pleasure. "Now if only I had my power back." She wanted to see his face and the look in his eyes. "Let me get you that towel you wanted." She moved carefully in the darkness toward the linen closet, toting Chloe on her hip.

"I sure could use it." He chuckled softly. "Because of the storm . . . ," he spoke loudly enough for her to hear him as she moved about the house, "the officers told me that this part of town won't have electricity until sometime tomorrow."

Returning with the fluffy towel and handing it Addison, Nina moaned. "What else can happen to me?"

"I want a drink, Aunt Nina," Chloe whined. The little girl rested her face next to Nina's and toyed with the soft curls of Nina's ponytail.

"Okay. Hold on," she said. She started toward the kitchen with Chloe clinging to her. She had only taken a few steps when she stumbled into the end table again. She howled with pain.

Addison's hands were on her shoulders. He guided her to the sofa. "Sit. I'll make this trip. Which way is the kitchen?"

"Straight to the back and make a right," Nina directed. "I have some small bottles of water in the fridge."

Watching his silhouetted frame moving carefully through the darkened house, Nina thought of the inconvenience the lack of electricity would cause her. She yearned for a hot shower, and there were two days' worth of dishes she hadn't done. She was suddenly full of shame at the thought that Addison would find how cluttered her kitchen was—how messy her whole house was. Living alone and often rushing off to the hospital, she did not worry about being a perfect house-keeper. She was grateful that the lights were off.

Chloe shifted on Nina's lap, squirming until Addison returned and handed her a small plastic bottle of water. "Thank you," she lisped.

Nina helped Chloe pull away the strip around the bottle top. "Have a seat, Addison. Take a breather from all you've done for us."

"I'm soaked from the rain. I don't want to ruin your furniture."

"Don't worry about it. I'm not that fussy. Join us on the sofa. We'd enjoy your company."

He took the towel, which he'd draped around his shoulder, and placed it on the cushion of the sofa. Then he sat beside them. His arm rested behind Chloe's back. He touched Nina on the shoulder to get her attention. "Why don't the two of you come and stay at my place? I have plenty of room, so you'll have your privacy. I would love to have you ladies as my guests." His voice was full of warmth.

"Oh, Addison, that's so kind. But really, we can make out now that Earl is out of the way."

"Turn on the lights, Aunt Nina," Chloe demanded between slurps of her water.

"She must think we're playing a game with this lights out stuff," Nina said. She patted Chloe's knee. "The lights can't be turned on for a while, honey. The electricity is not working because of something the lightning did."

"I hate the dark. Something is going to get me. Turn on the lights," Chloe said in an anxious whine. She began to rock back and forth.

"Nina, come to my house. The kid has been through enough for one day. We all have." His hand was on Nina's shoulder, squeezing it gently to persuade her.

Her flesh tingled deliciously where he had touched her. She liked the idea of him wanting to watch over her. She was used to men who took an interest in her only for her medical opinions. She was quite aware of the fact that she wasn't the kind of woman men were attracted to. She didn't flirt or play the kinds of roles men liked women to play to make them feel strong and brighter. Having been alone for most of her life, she was used to dealing with the daily challenges. However, the new responsibility for Chloe made her feel vulnerable. She wanted to do what was best for the little girl. And it was a relief, knowing she didn't have to face one more of life's trials alone.

"I suppose it'll be best for Chloe. It's really kind of you to go out of your way like this."

"It's my pleasure," he said.

Nina liked the sound of his response. It revealed warmth, and was probably accompanied by one of his wonderful smiles that she couldn't see in the darkness.

Chapter V

"I should buy you a steed and a suit of armor," Nina said to Addison on the ride to his place.

"Hmm . . . I don't think that's my style. I'll settle for dry clothes." He chuckled, keeping his eyes on the traffic, which had slowed because of the steady downpour. "What made you say that?"

"I just remembered. This is the second time you've come to my rescue," she said. She turned in her seat to study his profile.

"The second time?" He glanced at her, his voice filled with curiosity.

She reached into the back seat to reprimand Chloe for trying to undo her seatbelt. "Yes, it's the second time. The first time was years ago, when we were in high school."

"That's right, you did tell me we attended Dubois together," he said matter-of-factly as he switched lanes. "Did you graduate with me?"

"No, I didn't. I was a freshman when you were a senior."

"Oh. I suppose that's why I don't remember you," he said in a courteous yet disinterested tone. "How in the world did I save you? I may have been many things in high school, but heroic wasn't one of them."

Her heart squeezed in misery. He had not remembered one iota of the incident that had been so precious to her all these years! He might as well have been telling her that she hadn't been worthy of his remembering.

"Well, are you going to tell me? If I did something wonderful for *you*, I sure want to know about it." He pulled up to a stop light. He glanced her way, but his interest didn't seem genuine. "Come on. Out with it, Nina."

She hesitated. She wished she hadn't brought up the subject. He'd probably think the occurrence ridiculous. Men and women viewed incidents differently. Men didn't hold onto and treasure certain memories the way women did. "You kept some thugs from taking advantage of me," she said. "You pulled up in that fancy red car you had in high school and parked and blew your horn until the guys ran away."

"I did that?" He frowned as though he were trying to dredge up the memory.

"You even got out of your car and helped me off the ground. You drove me home, then you waited in your car until I was inside the house."

"Well, I'll be. Are you sure that was me?"

"Of course I'm sure. I've never forgotten it," she said softly.

"What kept us from becoming friends after that?"

"Oh, I wanted to be your friend. But I was a shy fifteen-year-old girl who could barely say hello to the most popular boy in school. Then you had that snooty girlfriend, the homecoming queen, who was always at your side. I was afraid that she would make me feel two feet tall if she caught me trying to be friendly with you."

"That was Deidre." He smiled dreamily. "She was something else. I broke off with her because she was so possessive. So jealous."

"Oh yeah, you were the man back then," she said with a tinge of bitterness.

"I still don't remember you or that little stunt. I really wish I did, though."

Nina let the subject go. It was pointless to make him remember or see how he had affected her life. She'd placed him on a pedestal, only to find that he no longer resembled the caring, sensitive boy he had been in high school. Until tonight, that is.

He pulled into the driveway of his place. "Here we are," he announced. "Boy, this rain isn't letting up." He hopped out of the car and grabbed his umbrella. He assisted Chloe out of the backseat and picked her up. She was delighted to be shielded by his oversize umbrella.

He tapped on the car window on Nina's side. "C'mon. There's plenty of room under here for you, too. Right, Chloe?" He beamed at the little girl.

Nina gave him a forced smile before exiting the car to be with them. She felt foolish for telling him about his rescuing her years ago. He hadn't even pretended to care what his gallant action had meant to her.

Huddled together under the umbrella, they dashed for his building in the downpour. While he changed out of his wet clothes, Nina and Chloe checked out his guest room. Then they looked at several other rooms, finally ending up in the rec room, where they found him on the phone.

"The food—pizza—is on its way," he declared, hanging up. He looked relaxed and handsome in the jeans and the denim shirt he'd changed into. He rubbed his hands together and grinned like an overanxious schoolboy, matching the excitement in Chloe's eyes. "We'll be eating soon, angel."

"Yeah!" Chloe clapped and let out a joyous shout, bouncing on his plush, sand-colored sofa. "Turn on the television," she urged, tugging on one of her braids.

"You've got it." He sat on the arm of a chair, picked up the remote control, and flipped on the set.

Chloe scooted toward him and leaned on his knee.

"Let's find something funny for you to watch," he said. "I doubt that there'll be any cartoons on at this hour, you little night owl." He tickled her side.

Chloe giggled. "What's a night owl?"

"You're a night owl. Up at all hours of the night," he teased her.

Moving toward the kitchen, which opened into his rec room, Nina watched Chloe and noticed the gleam in the child's eyes. She realized that Chloe was another victim of his charm. He certainly had a way with women, from eight to eighty. Nevertheless, she was impressed by how he had gone out of his way to make the little girl feel special. She had to admit that she was surprised by how good he could be with children.

"I finally found something interesting and appropriate for her to watch," he said, entering the kitchen.

"You've been a big help to me. I don't know how I'll ever repay you."

"I could think of a couple of things." An eager look came into his eyes.

She felt a lurch of excitement within her, then a warning voice calmed her down. "I bet you could. But I'm not interested in the kind of games you'd like to play."

His gaze traveled over her face and searched her eyes. "Nina, stop acting like a steel maiden. I bet you could be a live wire with a man if you could just stop being so . . . so tense . . . so serious."

"I could be. But you'll never have the chance to know." She smiled at him guardedly.

"Is that a challenge, sweetheart?" he asked. His brows lifted with amusement at her prissy attitude.

"No way." She shifted in her seat and refused to be hypnotized by the twinkle in his eyes. Her heart thumped hard and her nerves jangled. Agreeing to spend the night at his place, she'd had no idea that he'd make advances toward her. Was he serious, or was he only trying to see how far he could get with her? she thought. He probably assumed that she'd be a pushover because of her lack of male companionship. She tried not to give him the satisfaction of seeing how he affected her. She said one thing, but her body came alive with his flirty glances and his verbal come-ons.

He laughed wickedly and walked toward the refrigerator. "I'm going to prepare a salad for us." He retrieved lettuce, carrots, radishes, and a cucumber from the fridge and placed them in the sink.

"I love your house. Condo?" Nina asked. She was anxious to change the subject. She was growing tired of his frivolous flirtations. "I walked through it while you were changing clothes. I hope you don't mind."

"No problem. I'd like for you to see my bedroom as well." He flashed her a lecherous grin.

"I will, when you're not in it." She smiled sarcastically. "But this place is cozy and homey. Nothing at all like what I'd pictured you owning." His home was decorated with bright, contemporary furniture, lots of plants, and beautifully framed paintings by prominent black artists.

"And exactly what kind of home did you think I'd have?"

"Oh . . . well . . . nothing like this." She didn't want to reveal the fact that she'd imagined him to have a huge bed and mirrored ceilings right in his living room, and even in his rec room.

He wiped his hands on a dish cloth. "Perhaps you thought I'd live in something that looked like a brothel—satin, velvet, and plenty of black leather—with mirrors on the ceiling." He stared at her with a smile, the corners of his mouth twitching.

She tried to manage a straight face. She didn't want him to see that she had indeed imagined such things.

"Yeah, I can see I'm right." He laughed softly. "You've been listening to hospital gossip."

"Okay, so I'm guilty. I don't plug my ears when the gossips get to buzzing on the grapevine." She laughed softly and watched him put together the salad.

"Shame on you, Nina. I thought you were above that kind of thing." He chuckled. "But there are some juicy morsels on that grapevine." He smiled at her, reaching for a bottle of wine and two small goblets.

"By the way, how's the work coming on that money pit of a house of yours?" he asked. He seemed to be aware of her discomfort at his question. He handed her a glass of wine. "I'm sorry for the way that came out. Don't take it the wrong way. I wasn't trying to put you down or anything."

She tasted the wine, savoring the exquisite flavor. Of course, country-club Addison wouldn't buy cheap grocery store wine like she did.

"No offense taken." She wasn't going to let him see that he had insulted her by calling her home such a thing. It didn't matter what this rich boy thought of her or her house, she tried to convince herself. He wasn't aware that it took more than a doctor's income to live the way he did. He had family money to afford him the kind of comforts he took for granted.

"You must have sunk a fortune into that old place. But I imagine it's a nice starter house for someone like you. It'll probably have good trade-in value when you're ready to move."

"Yes, it's a very good investment for someone like me. It's my home. I'm not planning on moving any time soon," she said emphatically.

"Oh, I see." He looked as if he realized he had put his foot in his mouth again. He cleared his throat. "No offense, but I wouldn't want a woman of mine living in that place. There are some horrendous things happening on your side of town."

"Well, I'm not your woman, so you have no worries," she snapped. "I'm aware of the crime there. I'm not naive. Isn't crime everywhere these days? You could even have freaks living next door to you in this ritzy area."

"That's true. But at least I'm a man who can look out for himself."

She felt a twinge of embarrassment. "I'm not going to get into a thing with you about that. I don't have a leg to stand on, since you had to come to my rescue tonight."

"Exactly." He beamed, clearly pleased that his point had been validated.

"Okay," she said, annoyed that he had one up on her. "Back to the subject of my neighborhood. You don't know anything about the people there. I'm not afraid of them. I'm friends with them, and they respect me. There are still a lot of good, hard-working people in the area. You'll never hear about them, though. You won't hear about the clean lives they live, the good kids they've raised who have wound up being successful adults, and the good deeds they do."

"All right, already," he said. "Geez, you don't have to get on your soapbox." He touched her hand. It seemed like a gesture of understanding.

His display of sensitivity touched her. She took a sip of her wine before speaking. She hadn't expected his empathy. "I'll let you in on a little secret, since you offered hospitality to Chloe and me. My place once belonged to my parents. I have some great childhood memories there."

"Well, that explains everything. It makes more sense to me why you would live in that gloomy, run-down area."

71

"Addison, please."

"Sorry. Again, I meant no harm." He swigged his wine. "I sort of remember that section used to be nice. My mother had a housekeeper who lived in that area. I can't remember the street or anything. I was only four or five."

"I bet she was a good worker, and a good person too. Especially if she lived where I did then."

"I suppose. The only thing I remember is that she made the best chocolate chip cookies and the most delicious sweet potato pie." He sipped his wine thoughtfully. "So where do your parents live now?"

She rubbed the back of her neck, feeling the familiar sinking of loneliness. "They're dead," she said finally. "My father died on a construction job. My mother passed on a few years after him from a heart attack." She cleared her throat as a lump of emotion welled there unexpectedly. "When I returned from medical school in D.C. to Harper Falls and saw that our old house was up for sale, I had to have it. I didn't care that it was falling apart. I had to have it. It's my way of being close to them." She spoke softly, recalling the old days. "They were good people, too. They were all the family I had."

"You have no other relatives?" He wrinkled his brow in concern.

"None." She hated the look of pity that replaced the sparkle in his eyes. "Don't look at me that way," she said defensively. She didn't want him, of all people, to feel sorry for her. "I'm far from being a charity case. I've done quite well, don't you think? I have good friends to turn to in an emergency. Friends can be more priceless than money. But I suppose you already know that."

He nodded. "How long have you been without your folks?"

She heaved a sigh. She was reluctant to answer him. "I . . . I've been alone since I was twelve years old."

"You were raised in foster care, then."

"Yes . . . yes, I was."

"I'm sorry. That must have been awful."

"I learned more than I needed to know about the cruelty of people. But I'm still here." She brightened. "However, I try not accentuate the negative things in my past. I'm a survivor of Harper Falls' magnificent social services."

A silence fell between them.

Nina moved from her seat to check on Chloe, who was engrossed in a rerun of the show "Happy Days." She lay on her tummy, mesmerized by the antics of "the Fonz." Nina smiled and returned to the kitchen, reluctant to disturb the little girl.

"I wonder what happened to the pizza guy?" Addison glanced at his watch as she returned to her seat at the counter. "Everyone must be ordering pizza tonight." He grinned awkwardly at her. Clearly, he wanted to say something meaningful after what he'd learned about her. But obviously he was afraid that whatever he said would be misconstrued.

Oh no, he's feeling sorry for me, she thought. She didn't want or need his pity. She quickly moved on to another topic. "Now, your parents have a beautiful home," she said. The sprawling, two-story mansion in the Hubbard section was a showplace. She had often passed it in her travels.

"It's a great house. That place has been in my family forever. It belonged to my great-grandparents. Of course, my mother has renovated it several times over the years to suit her changing moods."

"After I lost my mother, I used to fantasize about living in a mansion one day. I thought some rich, lonely couple would find me fabulous and adopt me. I dreamed of having a spacious bedroom with a canopy bed, with wallpaper and draperies that matched." A wistful look came into her brown eyes.

She remembered the hours she had spent as a teen, hiding out in the public library, getting away from the unwelcome atmosphere of whatever insensitive family the state had placed her with. After she had completed her homework, she would spend time poring over fashion and home-decorating magazines. She'd daydream about the great clothes she would wear and what her life would be like with a husband and children . . . in a house with rooms that looked like the ones in the magazines.

Lost in her thoughts of the past and the big houses, she came out of her fantasy to find Addison studying her. "Just a silly kid dream," she said, suddenly feeling vulnerable because she had opened her heart to him. She shifted her eyes away from his.

The doorbell saved her with its impatient chiming. She was thankful to have Addison's attention drawn away from her.

"Pizza man!" Chloe exclaimed, bolting off the chair and dashing for the front door.

* * * * * * * * * * * * *

Once they had stuffed themselves, Chloe yawned loudly and rubbed her eyes.

"I'm going to tuck this child in," Nina said. "She should have been asleep hours ago. It's nearly midnight." She took Chloe's hand. "Say thank you and good night, Chloe."

Chloe dropped Nina's hand and rushed over to Addison, offering him a hug. "Thank you, doctor."

He beamed. "You're welcome, sweetheart. Sleep tight."

Chloe returned to Nina's side, accepting her hand.

"Nina," Addison called from the kitchen. "Come back and keep me company. Have another glass of wine with me. We can relax, talk in the living room."

"As soon as she's settled, I'll be back." She smiled and vanished into the guest room with the little girl.

Moving into the living room, Addison rubbed his hands together and grinned. He went to the CD player and programmed it to play some of his favorite romantic ballads. He smiled, dimmed the lights in the room, and fluffed the pillows that accented the spacious, comfortable sofa. He unbuttoned a few buttons on his shirt and prepared a tray for the wine and some snacks. He stared toward the guest room door, impatient for Nina's return. He pulled open the drawer of the end table near the sofa to see if there were condoms, and was pleased to find several in the small box there.

"She fell asleep almost as soon as her head hit the pillow," Nina said, coming into the room.

He shoved the drawer shut. He didn't want her to see what was in there. Had she seen the little box, he was sure she would have become offended and shut herself up in his guest room with the door locked.

He gave her his warmest lady-killing smile. "She's been through quite a bit. Poor kid." He patted the cushion beside him.

Nina took his offered glass of wine and sipped before settling near him. She noticed how soft the lights were and how romantic the music was coming from the sound speakers. Was he planning on seducing her to pass the evening? she thought. Was this compensation for giving her the use of his place?

Leaning toward her, he touched her shoulder. "Too bad about that Earl guy and how the storm blew out your power. But I couldn't have gotten you here any other way." He placed his hand on the back of her neck. "Tonight, I hope you've found something to like about me."

She studied the wine in her glass. She didn't want him to see the desire that she was certain was clear in her eyes. Yes, she had been defensive and cool with him every chance she got. It was easier to keep him at a distance. She didn't want to know that he wasn't attracted to her. Whenever she was around him, she felt even more plain and ordinary compared to his stunning good looks.

"Don't look so frightened," he said. "I'm not going to do anything to harm you. And I certainly wouldn't do anything that doesn't feel right to you."

Her mouth felt dry, and her stomach quivered deep within her. She couldn't believe that after all these years, she was alone with Addison. And he was hinting at a romantic interlude. He was more serious than earlier in the evening, when he had casually flirted with her and made her feel uneasy. But now that they were alone, she felt sure that he had an interest in her. It thrilled her that he could want her.

Sliding closer to her, he placed his arm around her shoulders. He used his other hand to turn her face toward his. His mouth covered hers in a lingering, hypnotic kiss.

The moment his lips met hers, she sighed and surrendered to the delicious heat that traveled from the top of her head to the tips of her toes—an awesome feeling for a woman who'd never known she could feel this way.

As the kiss ended, Addison gazed at her. His eyes smoldered. He licked his bottom lip as though he were still tasting the honey of her mouth. "I liked that," he whispered. "How about you?" He ran his finger down the bridge of her nose.

She was a bundle of excitement. Newly kindled sensations welled up within her, making her feel drugged. She wanted him to kiss her again. Her gaze focused on his mouth. Then she closed her eyes to send the message.

Addison scooped her into his arms, holding her body to his.

This time, she felt the breath leave her body from the splendor of his kiss and his bold desire for her. Heat settled in her center, making her moist and more stimulated the longer he kissed her. He slipped his hand beneath her shirt and bra, seeking the flesh of her breasts. Finding her hardened nipple, he thumbed it. She moaned and pressed her quivering thighs together to intensify the new thrills.

She wanted to tell him that she was a virgin. But she was caught up in the passion and afraid that he'd stop lavishing her with his touch and his kisses. They electrified every fiber of her being. She had never been this intimate with a man. She had made her ambition and her career her lover. She'd sublimated all her energy into those things, because they were the only guarantees she had in her life. But she'd always dreamed of having Addison as her first lover. She had never guessed it would become an actuality.

In a trance from his ardent affection, she obeyed his coaxing and stretched out on the sofa. He continued his passionate touching and kisses. She didn't protest a bit when he lay on top of her. It was a cozy feeling; it felt natural and wonderful in this magical moment. The bulge of his arousal pressed against her mound, radiating heat through her clothing. That same heat settled in her passion flower, making her restless and eager for what more was to come. He slipped his tongue between her lips and into her mouth. He probed her mouth, teasing her with silken strokes. She arched her body upward toward him. His breath was deep and hot as it fanned across her ear. The sound sent shivers up her spine.

Dazed by her new feelings, she allowed him to lift her top over her heaving breasts and discard it, then remove her bra. He fondled her globes like ripe, juicy apples. Then he lavished hot kisses on her breasts. Her body burned feverishly. In a cloud of passion, she breathed out great sighs of delight.

Surprisingly, she felt no shame at being half-naked. His eyes glowed with such desire that she wanted to explode with joy. This was the way she had always wanted it to be. She was a willing student to his masterful lovemaking. He amazed her with his knowledge of all the right spots to touch—sensitive spots that thrilled her. She gasped as he ravished her proud nipples with his flickering tongue and then sucked on them as though he were being nurtured. She abandoned herself to the tantalizing sensations. She had never expected to know such divine pleasure in her life.

She felt him lifting her skirt to tug away her panties. His hands wandered over her body in a slow journey and landed on her mound. He teased her sticky wetness, sliding his fingers inside her. The sensation was marvelous. She whimpered softly.

"You're beautiful," he said. His voice was husky with desire. He tore away his shirt, then his jeans and shorts.

In the dimly lit room, she admired his sculptured body; his magnificent erection made him even more gorgeous. At last her curiosity about his ability as a lover would be satisfied. Her heart tripped double-time, now that the moment of reckoning had arrived. Though she was a virgin, she was not naive about the mechanics of sex—not in her profession.

Leaning over to kiss her lips, he eased his body onto hers. The feel of his warm flesh on hers set her senses spinning. She wrapped her arms around his shoulders and kissed him with confidence to show him that she was ready. Yes, she was nervous—but she wasn't afraid. She expected his entry to be painful. Her main fear was that she might not please him. She wanted him to be enraptured by her. She wanted this to be the beginning of something that would last forever.

He paused briefly to sheathe his pride with a condom. Then he wedged his knee between her thighs to part them so he could bury himself within her feminine essence. His eyes flew open when his entry wasn't as effortless as he had anticipated. She watched the muscles in his jawline flex with his anxiety. Panting, he gazed into her eyes.

"Nina, you're a virgin?" He frowned in disbelief.

"Yes," she whispered in a breathy tone. "But don't stop. I don't want you to stop."

He closed his eyes and grunted. For a moment she thought that he might end the sweetness she'd been anticipating. He kissed her. "I won't hurt you." He said the words as though they were a prayer.

As she felt his taut manhood glide inch by inch further inside her, she held her breath in expectation of the impending pain.

Thrusting and withdrawing his hips gently to give her pleasure as far as he could go for the moment, he sighed and finally pushed hard enough into her to tear the shield of her virtue. He almost lost his restraint. The sight of her wincing touched him in a way that made him feel guilty and unworthy for what he had done.

Her body stiffened at the sharp pain. She had become a woman at last, she thought, as tears of joy misted her eyes. She would never forget this precious moment—or the man to whom she'd chosen to give her special gift.

"It's all right, baby," he said. "It will be sweet from now on." He licked her nipples and raised his body to hover over her and to ride her slow and easy. He wanted the rest of the journey to be rapturous.

A sudden release of abundant happiness welled up in her breasts with the thrill of his passion rod, gliding in and out in such a wondrous tempo. Gradually she felt her blood sizzling with a strange and lush feeling. She placed her arms around his neck, pressing her body to his lean contours. Soon he thrust into her as though he were possessed. Seeing his face contorted in heavenly agony, she gripped his tight bottom and ground into him with all her might. As he jerked violently with the release of his honey, she clung to him, trembling. Seized by the exquisite power of her body, her womanhood, she shuddered in his arms for what seemed like forever. Her moans and his grunts of ultimate satisfaction filled the night and soothed her soul.

Lying together in the afterglow of their lovemaking, Addison kissed her over and over. "You were beautiful. You sure were no bashful virgin. You were wonderful."

"I've waited for this moment—and a man like you to make it perfect. Special," she said, smiling with her newfound joy.

Her eyes sparkled with excitement. Now she could consider herself a complete woman. And she had been taken by the one man she'd always dreamed of having. She hugged him and kissed his forehead as he drifted off to sleep. She wanted no one but him to be her lover, she thought, as she too was overcome by the draining drug of satisfied passion. Her eyelids felt heavy. Her body was at peace. She surrendered to sleep.

* * * * * * * * * * * * *

She awoke in the morning to find her nude body covered with an afghan. She smelled coffee brewing in the kitchen. Addison must be preparing breakfast, she thought. Humming the melody from a love ballad that had played during their interlude, she slipped into her clothes, which she found lying neatly on the end of the sofa. Once she was dressed, she ran her fingers through her hair and walked toward the kitchen, anxious to see her lover's face. She wanted to see if he felt as glorious as she did.

As she neared the kitchen, she heard him on the telephone. "I'm sorry about last night, angel. Something came up that I couldn't help."

Horrified, Nina tiptoed closer to the door.

"Don't be mad at me," he said. "I'll make it all up to you tonight. I'll be all yours. I want you to wear that see-through number I gave you on our last trip out of town." He listened in silence for a moment, then chuckled. "Oh, baby, don't tell me stuff like that now. You must want me to come through this telephone line to get to you." He laughed. Cradling the phone near his ear, he walked toward the coffeemaker.

As he turned to reach for his coffee mug, he caught a glimpse of Nina storming away toward the guest room. He wondered how much she had heard. Hearing the bedroom door slam, he shook his head at his own stupidity. Why hadn't he used the phone in his bedroom? He cursed himself silently.

"Damn." He jammed his hand into the pocket of his bathrobe. Nina was a sweet, fresh piece. He would have to kiss her behind to get another chance to taste her. But, he thought with confidence, he could get her again. He knew what to say and what to do. There was nothing a woman liked better than a little drama. He took a deep breath to continue his conversation—his flirting with the female on the other end of the line.

Chapter VI

"Breakfast," Addison called as he tapped on the guest room door.

"Okay. Thank you," Nina answered in a forced, cheery tone. "We'll be out in a few minutes."

She bristled with anger. How dare he have a flirtatious conversation with one of his vixens while she was in his house? And after last night, no less! She tried to keep her rage and humiliation at bay while she helped Chloe dress. She didn't want to pull Chloe into the negative emotions coursing through her at the moment. He had cheapened the whole experience. Instead of allowing her to bathe in the glory of her rite of passage, he had made her feel used—like a whore.

By the time they reached the kitchen, she could barely look at him or appreciate the care he had taken to prepare breakfast.

"It's all here, Chloe." Addison set two plates on the table. "Everything you told me you wanted. Scrambled eggs, crisp bacon, toast, and grape jelly," he said with a broad smile, pulling out a chair for his little friend.

Chloe grinned at him as though he were her hero. Then she went to work eating the lovely meal he'd cooked especially with her in mind.

Addison looked disappointed when he noticed that Nina wasn't impressed by his culinary efforts. She stared at the food; the sight of it nauseated her. After the lusty night they'd shared, he clearly expected her to be ravenous.

He eyed her with a wry grin. "No appetite?"

She shook her head and poured herself a cup of coffee, swallowing her anger.

He eased up behind her and placed his hands on her shoulders. "How are you this morning?"

"I'm fine," she snapped. She shrugged his hands off her and moved away from the table and him to the other side of the room, carrying her coffee.

He looked bewildered. "Can I get you some coffee cake? It's fresh from the bakery."

"Nothing for me. I'm okay." She turned away from him and directed her attention to the morning paper, which lay on the counter.

"I'm not a breakfast person," he explained. "You girls help yourself to whatever you want. I'm going to shower and shave so that we can get out of here. I know you're anxious to get back to your place." He swung his attention from Nina's indifference to Chloe. It amused him to see her cherub face smeared with grape jelly. "You really do love that stuff, don't you, kid?" He chuckled softly.

Chloe munched on her gooey toast and grinned at him.

He winked at Chloe, then tried to read Nina's silence and cool body language. Damn! She *must* have heard him on the phone. And he cared more than he thought he would that she had. He felt like a thief for taking her virginity so casually. She'd saved herself for so long; she deserved to have lost her virtue to a better man—a more sensitive man than he. You're a real skunk, Addison, he thought.

Oh, but she had felt so sweet. She'd been so giving. His manhood throbbed as he remembered the soft sound of her sighs and the radiant glow on her face. He had to admit that last night he had viewed her as only another conquest in the beginning. But seeing the honesty of her emotions and her willingness to give that very precious part of herself had touched something in him that he had thought was dead. Their union had created a cocoon of bliss, pulling him into an ecstasy so heavenly that it had reminded him of what love used to feel like for him. He had awakened throughout the night with his nude body wrapped around hers. He had reluctantly disentangled himself without disturbing her sleep, lost in the wonder of this exquisite creature.

But with the morning had come reality. While he slipped into his robe, he had told himself that it was only sex—nothing more. He didn't want to fall in love. He didn't want to get caught up in the pain that always followed that deceptive, feel-good-all-over feeling love lured you into.

He cleared his throat to get her attention, but she paid him no mind. She continued to study the newspaper. He couldn't take her indifference. He was the one who usually dished out treatment like hers when he grew tired of a woman. "Uh . . . I'll be back after a while." He disappeared from the room.

She shoved the paper aside when she heard his bedroom door close. She dumped the remainder of her coffee into the sink, then picked up the phone and dialed the number of a taxi company from an ad in the newspaper that had caught her eye.

"Come on, Chloe. We're leaving." She wiped the child's face with a paper towel.

"But he's going to take us home now," Chloe said, looking at her in confusion.

She managed a bright smile. "No, we're going to take a taxi home. I thought it would be fun for you." I couldn't possibly spend another minute near this hypocrite, she thought. I don't need him or any of his help. By the time he's finished dressing, we'll be out of here. That way I won't have to hear any more of his lies.

Chloe's questioning expression switched to excitement. She hopped down from her chair and dashed into the living room, following Nina.

The moment Nina stepped out of Addison's place into the sky's yellow haze, she sighed. It was too fresh and sunny a day for her melancholy feelings. What a glorious day it could have been. If only he had been able to match the tender emotions she had offered him.

She was grateful to see the prompt appearance of the taxi coming toward her. The sooner she could get away, the better, she decided. As the taxi eased up to the curb and parked, Nina heard Addison call to her. She did not heed his call. She helped Chloe into the backseat.

Addison rushed up to her, dressed in jeans and tugging a grey t-shirt over his torso. He looked dismayed. "Nina, why are you leaving—and in a taxi? I was going to take you guys home."

"You've been too kind as it is," she said coldly. "We'll be fine." She flashed him an angry look.

He reached for her hand, but she snatched it away. He flinched as if she had hit him, then recovered himself. "About last night . . ." he said softly, staring at her with a tender look that was meant to melt her.

"Hey, last night is forgotten," she said, feigning friendliness. She caught his seductive look, but refused to succumb to it this time.

"We should talk . . ."

"There's nothing to talk about, okay? I had more than my share of wine. It made me . . . made me act irresponsibly." She pressed her lips in a tight line. "We both made a mistake. A big mistake." She climbed into the back of the taxi beside Chloe and slammed the door.

Addison leaned toward her window and tapped frantically on it. She ignored him and gave the driver her address—"1327 Marple Avenue."

Chloe turned on her knees to look out the back window. "Bye, Dr. Addison," she called, as though he could hear through the glass.

Nina heard the child, but she refused to look back.

"Will he come to see us tonight?" Chloe asked, settling down beside Nina on the seat.

"No, he won't. He has plans for tonight. He's a very busy man," she said, gazing pensively out the window. She'd heard him making a date with some hussy who was to play dress-up for him in some lewd sexual games.

"When will we see him again? He promised to take us somewhere fun," Chloe said.

Though the child's questions worked her nerves, she managed a smile. "We'll have fun. We have plenty to do to keep us busy." She squeezed Chloe's nose affectionately.

"Can we call him, so he can have fun with us?"

"No, Chloe," she said in a tone of finality. She'd had enough questions concerning Addison.

She didn't want to talk about him. She didn't want to think of him and what a fool she'd made of herself. She'd let down her guard and allowed him to seduce her. She'd gotten carried away with her fantasy. She'd offered him her virginity, thinking that this would impress him—this would let him know better than spoken words how much she cared for him.

After the tender love he'd made to her, she'd awakened feeling on top of the world. She had thought this day would be the beginning of something wonderful for her—for them.

Then she'd heard him on the phone. She hadn't even left the house before he was ready to make plans to be with another woman! She hadn't been special. She'd only been someone to pass the time—to satisfy his needs for one night.

She cringed inside when she thought of how he would probably laugh behind her back. She would become a bit of juicy gossip on the hospital grapevine. He'd probably brag to his friends that he had bagged the oldest living virgin. He probably felt as though he had done her a favor by relieving her of her chastity. Who else but the great womanizer, Addison Wagner, would want to have anything to do with the cold fish Nina was perceived to be?

Her feelings of shame turned to fury. She had lived her life being the butt of cruel jokes—once. Never again! It had been all wrong to dare to think—to dream—that she could have a place in his heart. To hell with Addison Wagner! He would never get close to her anymore. From this moment on, he would be nothing but another man who was unworthy of her attention. He would only be a professional associate—nothing more.

As the taxi pulled in front of her house on Marple Avenue, tears spilled from the corners of her eyes and met under her chin.

"What's wrong, Aunt Nina?" Chloe asked, frowning. She took Nina's hand as they scooted out of the taxi.

"Nothing, baby. I'm fine," she lied.

* * * * * * * * * * * * *

"Addison, you're slowing up, man," Doug Griffith panted. He was breathing hard after a vigorous game of handball. "I can't remember the last time I beat you."

Addison shrugged his shoulders and tore off the leather gloves he wore to protect his hands. He snatched the headband from his perspiration-drenched face. He trudged away from Doug toward his sports bag, lifted out a towel, and wiped the sweat from his face and around his neck. Then he reached for a bottle of water. He took a long swig, then turned toward the showers.

"So who's the latest honey in your life?" Doug asked, following him. His eyes lighted with excited anticipation. "Give me the usual details. She must be some spitfire. She's physically draining you, huh? That's probably why I beat you royally this morning."

"Doug, man, leave me alone. I'm not in the mood to entertain you."

"Bull!" Doug exclaimed. "You love letting me know what you do between the sheets—and with whom."

"Well, I'm changing my ways. I'm getting bored with those one-night stands."

Doug halted before they reached the locker room. "Oh, no, say it ain't so. Don't tell me that you've fallen in love."

Addison playfully smacked Doug on the back of the head and forced a chuckle. "Let's just say I'm becoming more responsible. Ever since my marriage ended, I've gone kind of crazy. I've used sex like an antidote to ease my pain. And it worked for a while."

"I thought Vanessa was out of your blood a long time ago," Doug said.

"She was. It's just that I refuse to be made a fool of again. I refuse to trust any woman with this heart of mine."

"You had no trouble sharing your love stick." Doug punched Addison on the shoulder.

"I have needs, brother. But I'm tired of sex without love. I want what you've got with Kimberly. A home and kids."

Doug screwed his face into a mock frown and placed his hand on Addison's forehead. "Are you coming down with something? This doesn't sound like my love-'em-and-leave-'em homey."

"Give me a break." Addison shoved Doug's hand away. He straddled the bench and sat down in front of his locker. "Wouldn't you like to see me settle down?"

"Yeah, man. Misery loves company." Doug laughed. Then he scratched the side of his face as though he were trying to figure out what had turned his friend around.

Addison felt like a lost soul. "Don't look at me like I've lost my mind. I haven't." He shook his head in dismay. "I don't like myself lately. I used to be a good guy, until Vanessa killed everything decent in me."

Doug plopped his stocky body down near Addison, staring at his friend. "Hey, man. Do you need a shoulder to lean on, instead of someone to fool around with?"

"I loved Vanessa with all my heart when I married her," he said hoarsely. Thinking of Vanessa reminded him of the vulnerability of that marriage—that union. "What a fool I was."

"I know that. I was there. I was the best man at that big extravagant wedding you two had," Doug said. "And you were one happy man on the day you said 'I do.'"

"It was supposed to last a lifetime. I thought I had the kind of marriage that her parents and my parents had." He got a sinking feeling from the memory of the tap dancing he had done to please and keep his beautiful wife.

When they had first married, he hadn't been able to spend much time with her. He was still in medical school and under a lot of pressure to succeed. But Vanessa had been an only child like he was; she was used to being pampered and given a lot of attention. She wasn't used to being supportive to anyone. She

89

and her needs had always been the center of her world. She felt neglected and couldn't understand why her husband couldn't alter his busy hospital schedule to suit her. She had no real idea of what was expected of her as a loving wife.

To ease his guilt for not being able to spend time with her, he had encouraged her to go out without him. He had encouraged her to take exotic vacations. Then he realized that was a mistake. She had taken a lover. His "perfect" wife had betrayed him. He cringed when he remembered that his credit cards and his money had financed their rendezvous. Though he had been hurt, he hadn't blamed her. He had blamed himself.

She had begged his forgiveness, and he had granted it. He loved her and couldn't imagine his life without her sophisticated flair or her elegant sense of style. What a snob he'd been, to let her superficial polish blind him to her selfishness.

When he'd finally graduated from medical school, he had tried his best to be the kind of husband she wanted. He had attended all the social events she loved. He had taken her on shopping sprees to New York and Los Angeles. They had even taken vacations to the Islands. It was a wonderful and romantic time for him. Their marriage was going to survive, he had believed.

Then, one day, he learned something that had nearly destroyed him. He and Vanessa had argued because he wouldn't be able to take her to Colorado on a skiing trip—not with a practice and several patients who required his attention. He had denied far too many career obligations in order to keep his wife happy and satisfied. He knew that he couldn't jeopardize his career any more than he had—not if he wanted to be considered one of the best internists. During the course of their altercation over the skiing trip, Vanessa viciously confessed that she was glad she had aborted his child. He wasn't worthy of a child from her! She had thrown the words in his face.

He had been stunned and shaken to the core. He had never been more heartbroken by anything in his life. The marriage had ended, and his heart had turned to stone. He had sworn never to love anyone again. He couldn't pay the price that loving too much cost. He had stuck by that vow—until he'd held sweet, dear Nina in his arms the other night.

"So you're ready to take that dive again," Doug said, breaking into his friend's thoughts. "Does she happen to be anyone I know?"

Addison shook his head and smiled cryptically. He dared not mention Nina's name. What was the use of talking about her when it was obvious that she now passionately disliked him? "There's no one in my life. I'm just thinking about it," he said.

"You're lying, but it's cool. I think I know who it is."

"You don't know a thing, man," Addison said, his sense of humor slowly returning. "Keep your nose out of my business. I'll let you know what's going on when I get straight." He glanced at his watch as he removed it to shower. "Look at the time. It's nearly ten o'clock. I'm expected at the clinic. I don't have any more time to mess around with you." He jabbed at Doug. "I'm going to hit the showers and get out of here. I'm supposed to be at the clinic within the hour."

* * * * * * * * * * * * *

Addison arrived at the free clinic to find it full. Rosie, the senior citizen volunteer receptionist, greeted him with a smile, then showed him a list of patients he had to see.

"Is Nina around?" he asked offhandedly. He had not seen her since she'd left his house a couple of days ago. He'd been busy at his practice. And when he'd tried to call her at the clinic or her office, she'd been unavailable to talk. He'd been told to leave a message if it was not about a patient.

91

"She's here," answered Rosie. "She's been busy as a bee all morning. She's in with a patient."

At that moment, Nina exited from an examination room with a young maternity patient following her.

As she approached the reception desk, Addison did a double take. In the last few days, she had made several major changes that enhanced her looks. She'd cut her hair, and she wore a hint of make-up.

"Good morning, Dr. Sterling," Addison said, leaning on the counter and staring at her warmly.

"Dr. Wagner." She greeted him as though he were a stranger. She handed her maternity patient a prescription for vitamins.

Addison couldn't take his eyes off Nina. She moved with a self-assurance he hadn't seen before. Her new look and her haircut made her look elegant and sexy. It emphasized how gorgeous her eyes were as well. He felt himself gaping like a teenager.

As though he were an obstacle, she scowled and reached in front of him to pick up the charts for her next two patients. He was hit by the gentle floral scent of her perfume. It intoxicated him. He wanted to compliment her new hairdo, but she breezed away from him before he could form the words without making a fool of himself.

He deserved the cool treatment he was receiving from her. What kind of man was he, to make a date with another woman with Nina still in his house? Had he done it because subconsciously he wanted her to hear? Had the honesty of her emotions and that night of lovemaking frightened him—reminded him of the commitment he thought he wasn't ready to make?

She had given herself to him as a gift, and he had rudely refused it. He couldn't get over the fact that she was still a virgin at her age. When he had first realized it in the heat of passion, he briefly had second thoughts. Yet he hadn't denied himself the opportunity of taking her—savoring the feel of her unleashed womanhood. It had excited him to be her first lover. A wave of shame pulsed through him. In the back of his mind, he had known her inexperience would make her want a commitment—something that had been far from his mind that night. He had only wanted casual sex—nothing more—but he had become the unwary hunter captured by the game. What a twist! Now he found himself sitting around reliving that beautiful moment and wondering what he could do to make her love him—or at least like him.

It had disturbed him to discover that Nina and Chloe had left that morning while he was showering. Women didn't walk out on him. He had spent the day in a rage of hurt pride.

But later, thinking it over, he had been haunted by the look on her face while he'd made love to her. She'd been so lovely— so exquisite. She'd given herself to him as though she was born to do just that. Hadn't she mentioned something about having a crush on him in high school? He rubbed his chin thoughtfully. He wished he could remember their conversation about this. Maybe he'd dig out his yearbook to see if he could spot her picture. It might jog his memory and remind him of the deed she had treasured through the years.

Nina returned to the reception desk, muttering about picking up the wrong chart.

Addison's heart turned over at the sight of her. "Nina, can I talk with you when you get a break?" He fell into step with her as she hustled back toward the examination room.

"Is it something about a patient?" She held the chart close to her chest, giving him a somber look he couldn't read.

"No, it's about us," he admitted like a awkward boy.

"Really, I don't have the time. There is no *us*." She attempted to push past him.

"Nina, you've got to hear me out," he said, blocking her path. "I want to talk about the other night. I don't want you to . . ."

"You don't want me to what? To feel like a whore? Or just another piece who was foolish enough to let you use me to while away the time and amuse yourself?" She gave him a hostile glare. "Get out of my face!"

Her unexpectedly scathing tone made him flush in shame. "Nina, I'm sorry. Just give me another chance . . ."

"Another chance? No, I don't think so." She grimaced. "I'm too smart to repeat a major mistake more than once." She held her head high with indignation. "Get out of my way! We have too many patients to waste time playing your kind of games."

Crushed, Addison stepped aside to let her march off. He deserved her contempt. He had no right to be close to her after having treated her like a piece of meat.

Slowly, he made his way to the reception desk to get the charts for the patients he had to see. He'd deal with Nina later. He would make her see that he was no longer the adolescent male he'd been behaving like. He'd find a way to show her he could be a real man. He'd make her see that he was the kind of man who could give a real woman like her the things that mattered in life—love and happiness. His soul wouldn't rest until he'd made that sweet woman his.

Chapter VII

Much to Nina's dismay, Jenny Martin developed pneumonia. Her punctured lungs had become congested, and she maintained a high temperature. As her physician, Addison decided to have her moved to the Harper Falls Medical Nursing Center. There she could receive the care she needed to regain her strength. Nina had no choice but to continue her guardianship of Chloe.

Chloe had been with her for a week, and in that time Nina had come to love the little girl's company. True, it was not easy carting her to day care and spending time preparing balanced meals for her. Nina had been fortunate enough to get Mrs. Wheeler, her neighbor, to sit with Chloe when she was awakened in the night to come to the hospital for deliveries.

Her biggest problem was still Earl. He had shown up at St. Luke's Hospital one day to visit Jenny. Nina hadn't wanted to pry, but the few words she had overheard proved to her that Earl was up to no good. He had sat by Jenny's bedside, holding her hand and persuading her that he was a changed man who was going to make her and Chloe's life better.

The day Jenny was transferred to the nursing home, Nina went to see her.

"Earl wants me to let Chloe stay with him," Jenny told Nina in a low, breathy tone. She lay propped up on pillows in bed in the nursing home.

"And what did you tell him?" Nina asked, sitting in a nearby chair. She smoothed the tapered back of her new hairstyle. She still felt self-conscious about her changed looks.

"I told him that Chloe was quite happy with you."

"Good. That child doesn't need to be with him."

"You know, he cried yesterday. He told me how lonely he was." Jenny fell into a coughing spasm.

"Has he stopped drugging and drinking?" Nina asked. She frowned in concern and poured water into a cup. She supported Jenny's shoulders with one arm so the woman could sip slowly. "When you are better, you should consider moving out on him until he gets himself together. The next time he loses his temper and gets to pounding on you, you could be even more seriously hurt than this awful episode."

"Nina, he's my man. He's not a brute all the time. He can be the sweetest man in the world when he's sober. He . . . he needs me to stand by him and to help. He told me he can do anything with me by his side. He's making arrangements for me to go to rehab with him."

"Rehab for you? You don't need rehab. He's the one with the problem. He ought to be there now—or in jail for what he did to you. If he cared for you and Chloe, he'd be getting treatment now." Nina couldn't believe how naive this woman was. What would it take for her to see that the man was a loser? "Besides, he has to lick his demons for himself, not for you."

96

Jenny coughed some more, wincing. She held her chest in pain.

"You need to concentrate on getting better for Chloe," said Nina. "Earl can look out for himself." She moved to the window, where she had a view of the garden and parking lot. "Has Dr. Wagner been in to check on you today?" she asked in a casual tone.

"No, he hasn't. But he'll be here, I'm sure. He saw me every day when I was in the hospital," Jenny said. A hint of a smile eased her darkened lips, still bruised after a week. "That's a fine man, Nina." She coughed again. "He's your type."

"No, he's not," Nina snapped. He'd proven to her by the way he used her that they had nothing in common."

"Oh, I see. I'm sorry. I wasn't trying to get in your business." Jenny grinned sheepishly. "How's my baby? You said you would bring her to see me."

"And I will. She's adjusted marvelously, but she misses you. Maybe day after tomorrow you'll be strong enough for her company. This is just your first day here. You need rest. That's most important for you right now."

A nurse entered the room to check Jenny's IV. Nina glanced out the window again. Clouds were beginning to roll in and hide the sun. She hoped it wouldn't rain. She frowned as she saw Earl's raggedy truck pull into the parking lot.

"Looks like you've got company," she said, annoyed, as she watched Earl hop out of his truck and march toward the nursing home. "I'm leaving." She gave Jenny's hand an affectionate pat, then moved to the door. She wanted nothing to do with that abusive little man. She prayed that by the time Jenny left the nursing home she would have the sense to leave him. She didn't want Chloe around such a mean-spirited man.

Earl accosted Nina in the hall. He stepped up to her and jabbed his finger in her face. "I'm sick and tired of you being in my business!" he bellowed. "I was just at the hospital, looking for my lady, and they told me she was moved here. Nobody said anything to me. And it's all your doing! Just because you don't have a man, you're trying to come between me and my Jenny. I won't have it, woman! You don't understand what she and I have. Stay out of my business!" His voice boomed throughout the hallway.

Nina glared at Earl and backed away from him. He reeked of liquor and weed, and he needed a bath in the worst way. "Lower your voice," she ordered. "I want you to carry your butt home to sleep off whatever it is you're flying on. Jenny can't take any stress. She doesn't need you in her face with all your empty promises."

He balled his fists. "I'm sick of you. You can't tell me what to do! I want my daughter. She's no kin to you. I'm her daddy. I'm going to get me a lawyer and haul you to court. I've got rights! I can take care of my family!" he ranted. He lunged toward Nina and grabbed her arm.

Suddenly, Earl was lifted off his feet. Addison, his eyes dark with fury, had hooked him in the back of the collar. "Hey, man," Addison growled, "you've got to go." He steered Earl roughly away from Jenny's room. "And I better not ever catch you bothering this lady or Chloe again."

"Forget you!" spat Earl.

Alerted by the commotion, two security guards appeared. They seized Earl, tussled with him, and moved him determinedly toward the door.

"I ain't seen my woman yet," said Earl angrily. "You ain't treating me right. You messin' with my family. Damn you!" he hollered over his shoulder as he was dragged out of the building.

Addison stood with his arms akimbo, watching Earl being taken away. "What a lowlife." He swung his attention to Nina. "You okay?"

She took a calming breath and nodded to reassure him.

"I worry about you and Chloe because of him. He's irrational, and he knows where you live." His piercing, concerned eyes pulled her into his gaze.

"We're fine," Nina said, looking away from him. She refused to let him see her anxiety. But she hadn't slept soundly since Chloe had arrived. The slightest sound would startle her and make her wonder if Earl was coming in to kidnap his daughter. She'd considered moving into a motel room until Jenny got out of the hospital. But with her condition, Jenny was going to be in the nursing home for at least two weeks, according to Addison's diagnosis. Nina had decided to live each day with prayer instead of living inconveniently in a motel.

"Come stay with me," said Addison. "You'll be safe there. The security is tight, and . . ."

"I don't think that's such a good idea. I might be safer with Earl," she said. *How dare he make such a suggestion?* she thought. He just didn't get it. Obviously his oversized ego wouldn't allow him to accept the fact that she refused to be his paramour.

Nina noticed how Addison flinched from her caustic words. The look on his face turned somber.

"Listen, I know I'm not winning any popularity contests with you at the moment," he said. "But there's Chloe's welfare to consider. I like the kid. I want to protect her as much from this situation as you do." He touched her shoulder. "Can't we call a truce for Chloe's sake and join forces? If anything happened to either of you, I'd feel responsible."

"Well, don't. You have your life, and I have mine. Besides, I'd rather dial 911 than call on you." She whirled away from him.

"Nina, wait. Don't be like this," he implored, trailing her. "Stay at my place. I won't bother you. I promise. This will be strictly a platonic thing. Okay?"

Nina remembered the look of venom on Earl's face and the way he had attacked her and blamed her for his family problems. Her worst fear was that he would take the child and leave town to punish her and Jenny for trying to outsmart him. However, she refused to stay with Addison. She'd rather take her chances. She had good neighbors whom she'd alerted about that lowlife, Earl.

"Thanks, but no thanks," she snapped. "I don't need you." She glared at Addison and rushed toward the exit.

Hitting the door that led outside, she was sprinkled by rain. She had no umbrella to shield her, but she didn't care. Tears washed down her face, blending with the raindrops. She hated herself for reacting this way to Addison. If she didn't care for him anymore, why was she still hurting from his humiliation— her broken dreams of a romance with him?

Chapter VIII

By the time Addison agreed to allow Chloe to visit Jenny, she had been at the nursing home for a week. He and Nina thought that the little girl needed to see her mother to quell any fears she had over her well-being.

Dressed in a new outfit to impress her mother, Chloe was as excited as though it were Christmas morning.

On the ride to the nursing facility, Nina thought about how much her life had changed since Jenny had shown up at the clinic. Her life had been a roller-coaster ride of emotions. She'd gone from being alone and lonely to a woman who'd been teased by love, tasted the responsibilities of motherhood, and experienced the pain and deception of romance.

"Chloe, my sweetie," Jenny said in a restrained tone that didn't match the joy in her eyes.

"Mama, I brought my coloring books like you told me over the phone." Chloe climbed up beside her mother.

It pleased Nina to see how Jenny perked up in her child's presence. She kept stroking Chloe's hair and rewarding her with kisses.

"I could hardly sleep last night, thinking about us being together." Jenny beamed at her daughter.

"Chloe has been just as excited," said Nina. "She was up at five o'clock this morning. I tried to get her to go back to sleep, but that was out of the question. She's been watching the clock to remind me of the time I promised to bring her."

"Don't tell me she's learned to tell time?"

"Yes, she has. I had to make her time-conscious because of my schedule. She's been a big help to me. She keeps me organized." Nina smiled at Chloe.

Jenny's eyes misted. "I don't know how I'll ever repay you. I know it hasn't been easy for you, and . . ."

"Let's not talk about that, okay? Chloe is a reward in herself. I'm going to miss her when you get back on your feet and take her home."

Smiling at her friend, Jenny turned her attention to the bright pictures that her daughter proudly showed her. She cooed her praise over all the colored pages Chloe pointed out to her. Chloe handed her mother some crayons and insisted that they color a picture together. Though weak, Jenny set to work. The child's warmth and nearness appeared to do more than any medicine had in the last few days, Nina thought.

In order to give the mother and daughter time alone, Nina wandered out into the hallway. There she saw Addison walking toward her. He greeted her with a quick smile. "How long has Chloe been with her mother?"

"We've been here nearly twenty minutes."

"Let's not wear Jenny out. Give them another ten minutes." He peered into the room to see Chloe and her mother, coloring and talking and giggling softly.

"Hey, I don't have any other plans after I examine Jenny," he continued. "How about you and me taking Chloe to the park for a little while? I came by there on my way here, and the playground was humming with youngsters." He slid a hand into his pocket and the other on his hip, lounging casually against the wall and waiting for her response.

She liked Addison's new attitude. She had to admit it to herself. This past week had been more pleasant than she would have guessed. He had begun to behave like the sensitive and caring guy she remembered from high school. It was a startling transformation. To her, those qualities made him more appealing than his macho, flirty posturing—the pose he adopted when he was near an attractive woman or attempting to intimidate her with sexual innuendoes.

"I know she will love it," said Nina. "I had no idea what to do with her once we left here. I'm expecting her to be tearful, having to leave her mother."

"I know she misses her mom, but maybe this park excursion will cushion her sadness," he said. He watched and listened to Chloe as she instructed her mother to stay inside the lines. He laughed softly. "I'd better go save Jenny. We don't want her to have a relapse because of poor coloring skills." He gave another chuckle.

Nina followed him into the room. "Chloe, it's time for us to leave. Your mother needs her rest, sweetheart."

"But we're having fun." Chloe leaned on her mother's chest.

"We'll come back in another few days," Nina said.

Chloe looked up at her mother. Her bottom lip quivered. "I want you to come with us."

"I'll be able to go another time." Jenny glanced at Addison. "I should be out of this place soon, huh, Dr. Wagner?"

"If you keep following my orders like you have, you should

be able to leave in a week or even less." He spoke to Chloe in a warm, professional tone. "She needs more rest and the medicine I've prescribed for her to make her all better." He cupped the little girl's chin. "Now, give your mom a big hug. The more rest she gets, the faster she can be with you. Nina and I are going to take you to the park."

"Wow, Chloe. You're a lucky little girl," Jenny said, hugging her daughter. "I want you to have a good time. Have an extra ride on a swing for me."

Chloe smiled. "Okay."

"You get some rest," Nina instructed. "Chloe will be fine."

"I see that she is. I appreciate the way both of you are taking her under your wing. What with Earl acting like a madman, it's a load off my mind. There's no telling who could have been near my child or where he would have taken her."

Addison took his stethoscope and placed it on Jenny's chest, then repeated the procedure on her back. "You sound much better today, Jenny. I want to keep you on the antibiotics for a few more days." He went to the foot of her bed where her chart hung to record his findings.

When Addison had finished his brief examination, Nina leaned over her friend and hugged her, as she always did after a visit. "Keep minding his orders. We're off to the park."

"I'll take two extra swings," Chloe promised her mother.

Nina grinned at Jenny and shook her head with amusement. They both knew that the child would wear her out long before the outing was done.

Jenny laughed until her laughter turned into a brief coughing spell.

"Sounds a lot better, Jenny," Addison said. "Make sure you drink plenty of fluids to clear up the phlegm in your lungs so you can expectorate it. I'll be in to check on you tomorrow." He sauntered toward the door. "I'll see you ladies outside. I have some orders to leave at the nursing station." He smiled at them and left the room.

"We'll call you later, Jenny," Nina said. She helped Chloe stack her books and crayons to end the visit.

"I'll color more pictures for you," Chloe promised, squeezing her mother's hand.

Jenny gave Nina a quizzical look. "By the way, is there anything going on between you and my doctor?"

"Now I know you're getting better." Nina placed her hands on her hips. "We're friends. Nothing more, okay?"

"If you say so." Jenny settled back on her pillow with an amused look. "You guys have fun."

"We will. Take care, hon." Nina took Chloe by the hand. The child waved playfully at her mother until they exited.

Addison was waiting for them beside his car. Jumping with excitement, Chloe allowed Nina to strap her into her seat and they set off. As they neared the park, they could hear the noise of kids at play; it was a loud sound, but pleasant. The children swarmed through the park like flies as they went from one plaything or play area to another.

"I want to go on the zig-zag sliding board!" Chloe exclaimed the moment they pulled into the parking area. She managed to release her seat belt in Addison's car without any assistance. She was on her knees in the backseat and trying to unlock the back door.

"Calm down, Chloe. We have the entire afternoon to spend in the park," Addison said, unlocking the back door.

Chloe hopped out of the car and lunged at him to let her pass. "I want to get on the slide." Her eyes gleamed with excitement as she glimpsed the tall sliding board in the nearby sandy field.

"We must be gluttons for punishment," Addison said.

"I'll say. Look at those kids. They have to get on everything here. The jungle gym, the swings, and that awful sliding board. It wears me out just looking at them."

He shook his head. "Now I understand why my married friends with kids have no energy for sex."

Nina laughed softly. His mention of sex didn't offend her. She realized with satisfaction that he wasn't trying to come on to her, just making a harmless comment. "Let's get going." She exited the car, scrutinizing the slide that Chloe seemed to love. It looked so high and scary that it made Nina nervous.

Addison held onto the squirming child, who was anxious to get away. "Whoa, there, honey!" he said.

"Chloe, I don't want you pushing and shoving on the other kids," Nina said.

"That's right. And don't try to act like you're an acrobat in the circus," added Addison.

"I know, I know," Chloe whined, focusing on the area where kids were lined up for their chance on the zig-zag sliding board.

"Let her go, Addison," Nina said, sighing.

Addison laughed and released the child. "Look at her go. She's a little dynamo."

Nina followed Chloe, keeping her eyes on her as the child fell into line at the slide.

Nina wrinkled her brow. "I don't like that thing. It's so high. When she gets to the top of it, I'll be afraid she's going to topple to the ground."

"That's the thrill of it, Nina. It's probably the most dangerous thing she's ever done. And kids know it makes their parents crazy. That's another reason for them to like it." He pointed toward a group of adults, parents of the other children. All the kids were about the same age as Chloe. "Not that you're the only one who looks nervous." His glance fell on Nina face, twisted with stress. "But she'll be fine."

Nina wasn't sure about that. She shielded her eyes from the sunlight as she watched Chloe climbing higher up the ladder to the chute. Three steps from the top, Chloe held onto the rail with one hand and wave enthusiastically to Nina.

"Oh, my goodness," Nina murmured. She feigned a smile and waved back. "I can't watch this." She turned away and folded her arms at her waist. "You watch her and tell me if she's all right."

"Zoom! There she goes." Addison laughed. "Her first mission is completed."

Nina turned in time to see Chloe sitting in the sand where she had landed from her ride on the board. The little girl bounded to her feet and brushed off her jeans bottoms, then headed for the end of the line.

"Oh no, not again."

"Now what made you think once was enough?" Addison teased.

Nina watched Chloe with the same anxious anticipation as she ascended the ladder once more.

Addison watched Nina. The last couple of days, he'd gotten more pleasure out of being with her than he had out of anything he'd done in years. And Chloe's being with them only added to his pleasure. Though he had promised Nina that he wanted to be no more than friends, he still hoped that this friendship would cause her to trust him again. He wanted her. The cooler she was with him, the more he wanted her. The one night that they had lain together in intimacy haunted him. He wanted to be inside of her. He wanted to feel her sweet warmth clutching his member with her yearning . . .

"Chloe!" Nina screamed and covered her mouth with her hand. Terror engulfed her as she watched Chloe drop from her high spot on the board ladder and hit the ground with a thud. For a moment Nina couldn't move.

"C'mon, Nina!" Addison shouted. Fear glittered in his eyes as he towed her from the spot where she seemed to be frozen. She began to pray for Chloe's well-being as she sprinted toward the area where the child lay motionless. All the kids halted their activities and hovered around Chloe in silence.

Seeing Chloe sprawled on the ground, Nina felt as though her heart were lodged in her throat. Although she was a physician, she found it difficult to remain calm. All her medical training couldn't rationalize away the fear she experienced, watching the little girl she'd come to adore in this unexpected trauma.

Reaching the child first, Addison dropped to his knees.

At first, Chloe appeared dazed. "Chloe, where are we?" Addison asked in a loud voice.

Nina knew Addison wanted to make sure that the child was coherent and didn't have any signs of a concussion.

Chloe's eyes fluttered, and she squinted at him. "Park."

"That's right. What day is this?" Addison made the child lie still while he checked her eyes and touched her gently to make sure there were no broken or sprained body parts.

"Saturday." Chloe wanted to sit up. She clutched her elbow, which was scraped and bleeding. "Aunt Nina, Dr. Wagner, look," she whimpered.

Nina was relieved that she recognized them. It was a very good sign. "I see, sweetheart," she said. "We'll get you all fixed up." Relief flooded her. Thankfully, the fall hadn't been a critical one. Suddenly she understood the anxiety that mothers experienced at times like these.

"That's right," Addison said. "I'll take care of that nasty cut."

"She fell on top of that boy," Nina explained to Addison, pointing to a chubby child. Nina was glad to see that the boy Chloe had fallen on was all right. He rubbed his behind, which had cushioned the little girl. He watched with the other curious bystanders.

Addison scooped Chloe from the ground. "Come on, let's take her over to that bench. I'll get my bag. I've got antiseptic and a Band-Aid."

Nina walked beside him, holding Chloe's hand to comfort her. She sat down on the bench and took Chloe on her lap.

"I want you to relax. It's okay," Addison assured Nina. He touched Nina's hand and smiled with beautiful candor.

This time she didn't resist his touch. She experienced that feel-good-all-over emotion she had tried to keep at bay since that night of failed bliss.

He gave her a swift, gentle kiss. "I'll be right back," he said to Chloe. His eyes met Nina's with a hopeful glint.

Watching him jog toward his car on the parking lot, Nina hugged Chloe, who held her arm awkwardly to examine her minor injury. Nina's heart tripped faster. She didn't want to pretend any longer that she didn't want him. She had grown tired of that game. He had persuaded her with his sincere kindness and interest for her and Chloe's welfare. Her heart swelled with joy and love. She wanted to laugh. She felt so good. The sparkle she'd seen in his eyes had said more than words. In the blink of an eye she'd seen love. She was certain that this time his feelings matched hers. She hoped with everything in her that his emotions for her were as real as hers had been for him, ever since that day he had become her hero.

* * * * * * * * * * * * *

Addison sat on the sofa in Nina's house, drinking beer. His feet rested comfortably on the coffee table.

"You would have thought she'd broken that arm instead of scraping it," Nina said, coming into the room. "I had to be very careful with it when I gave her a bath. The least touch, and you'd have thought she was dying."

109

"Did you put one of those cartoon Band-Aids on it? The ones we bought at the drug store?"

"I had to. She probably wouldn't be in bed asleep if I hadn't. She thinks it has healing powers."

Nina plopped down on the sofa next to Addison, folded her legs, and leaned toward him. She glanced at the news talk show Addison had been watching. She wanted his attention to be focused on her.

His arm went around her shoulder; he caressed her arm as though he'd read her thoughts. "Can you believe how we reacted to Chloe's incident?" he said. "Both of us are doctors, yet that playground fall scared us to death." He grunted softly.

"I'd never be able to forgive myself if anything happened to Chloe while she's with me."

"Accidents do happen. As her guardian, you're doing a great job. Looks to me as though you're going to make a great mom someday. You do want kids of your own, don't you?" He peered at her intently and brushed the side of her neck with his fingertips.

Meeting his gaze and feeling the tenderness of his touch, her heart turned over. "Yes, of course I want a family. . . one day. I miss having a family of my own. I look forward to that day when I can have the kind of love that comes from kin."

"Believe it or not, I can't wait to settle down and have a house full of children." He spoke in a lulling tone. He took her hand in his and turned it palm upward. He ran his fingertip back and forth on her flesh in a lazy manner.

The simple action set off sparks of desire. She recalled the intimacy they'd shared. He'd made her first time splendid— until he'd ruined the memorable event with his insensitivity. She removed her hand from his and sat up straight, holding her body stiffly.

"What's wrong, Nina?" His furrowed brow revealed how unnerved he was by the change in her mood.

She clasped her hands and held them beneath her chin, studying him. She wanted him, but she didn't want to be used as she had been the first time they shared a night of intimacy. "I suppose I'm just tired. Stressed. The last couple of weeks have been rough," she said. She rubbed the back of her neck, feeling it tighten with tension.

"Turn your back toward me," he instructed. "Let me pamper you, give you a massage."

She couldn't resist his offer. She shifted her body away from him. He began to work the top part of her shoulders with his strong hands and magic fingers. "Oh, that feels marvelous," she declared softly. Her body went limp and she closed her eyes to savor the heavenly sensation. The constant motion of his hands and fingers unleashed her tension.

When he stopped the massage, he pulled her against his chest. He held his face next to hers and caressed her arms. He kissed the side of her neck, making her shiver with delight.

Hypnotized by his warmth, her insides jangled with excitement. When he kissed the back of her ear, the unexpectedly delicious sensation caused her to jump away with a small cry of surprised pleasure.

"Come back, angel." He laughed at her reaction, turned her to face him, and enfolded her in his arms.

"I thought we agreed to be just friends." She looped her arms around his neck and gazed into his eyes.

He kissed her. "Tonight I want to be more than your friend." He angled his head slightly to fit her mouth more easily and gave her a deep, passionate kiss. When her lips parted and he tasted her sweet mouth, he sighed.

The sound of his satisfaction and the pressure of his lips, combined with the feel of his probing tongue, made her start trembling. "Do you think this is a good idea?" she asked in an almost inaudible tone between kisses.

"Yes. Oh yes, sweetness." He continued to seduce her with his wet and eager kisses. He slipped his hand beneath her top, seeking her heaving breasts. He fondled them as if they were precious gems.

His touch singed her and convinced her that what was occurring was indeed right. Her breath caught in her throat from the dizzying uprush of emotion. Then she exhaled and gave in to her pent-up passion. She relished the feel and the taste of his tongue. She burned for him and all that she knew he could do to satisfy her.

"Your bedroom," he murmured against her mouth, continuing his kisses and caresses.

She leaned away from him, giving him a smoldering look. Without saying a word, she rose from the sofa and extended her hand to him. He accepted it. They strolled into her bedroom as though they were walking on clouds.

Behind the closed door of her darkened room, they fell onto the double bed she'd never shared with any man. Rolling and tumbling from one side of the bed to the other, they tore away each other's clothes.

Sprawled on her back, Nina had no qualms about the way Addison's hands journeyed over her form. She writhed beneath his exquisite touch. Feeling his lips and his tongue tasting her nipples, she arched her body upward to him. Heat radiated from the core of her being and enflamed her heart, making it beat faster. As the thrills heightened, her passion flower moistened, aching to be filled with his member.

Straddling her, he hovered above her, kissing her and nibbling on her lips until she could barely breathe. All the while, she felt his erection grazing her thigh. Its pulsating heat fanned the fires of her growing desire.

Caressing the curves of her waist, her hips, and her luscious thighs, he could no longer withhold his desire to be inside her. He parted her legs and ran his hand over her moist mound. He fingered it as if he had found honey. Then he slid deep inside her with perfect ease. He groaned from the sweet, sticky warmth of her. He paused a moment to savor this thrill and to restrain his anxious member. Then he set a rhythmic tempo that she fell into with the sway of her hips.

In a mist of ecstasy, she clung to him. He made her feel like a beautiful rose blooming under the sun. She loved the way her hardened nipples pressed against his chest. She loved the feel of his manhood pushing in and out, making her body glow with warmth and tingle with excitement. She whimpered with the delight of his sincere passion. When he drove faster and harder inside her, she flung away her last shred of resistance. Her veins sizzled and her core throbbed with ferocious pleasure. She rocked against his unrelenting thrusts. Holding onto him, she felt his flesh as fevered as her own. Soon they were straining against each other, groaning and moaning with the beginning of their climax. The last delicious, shuddering moments came on them simultaneously. He collapsed upon her heaving breasts to share tender kisses and the happiness of their splendid union.

In the slow, cooling aftermath of their lovemaking, they snuggled beneath the covers, clasped together as though they would never be parted.

"I wish we didn't have to leave this room," said Addison. "Everything is so uncomplicated and simple between us." He kissed her shoulders slowly and tenderly.

Though Nina's body hummed with the rapture she'd found in his arms, she knew she had to be careful. As far as she knew, what had happened between them could be nothing more than great sex for him. The last time they'd been together, she'd been foolish enough to believe that their intimate interlude would begin something special and wonderful between them. She turned to face him. She stroked his face with the back of her hand.

He removed her hand and kissed it in a courtly manner. "Can I be your hero again? Will you be my lady?"

He said all the right things. He had done all the right things that a man does to charm a woman. Still, she wasn't ready to give in to the intoxication of her body and her spirit. Before she made such a commitment, she wanted to be sure that he cared for her sincerely. She didn't want a relationship built on sex alone.

"I do like you a lot," she said. "But I'd like for us to slow things down."

"You still don't trust me, huh?"

"I didn't say that." She snuggled closer to him.

"If it's time you need, then you can have it. I'm not going anywhere. No one else interests me." He slid his arm around her shoulders and held her. "You'll see that I'm not playing games with you."

His declaration seemed sincere, she thought, enjoying his masculine warmth between the sheets. However, the sting of her humiliation and embarrassment was still fresh. She remembered all too well what had happened the last time she'd placed high expectations on a relationship with Addison. Before she gave her heart and soul to him, she wanted to be absolutely sure that he wasn't going to toy with her delicate emotions.

Chapter IX

Addison knew when his mother called his office to request he come to the house that it was going to be more than a social visit. He could hear it in her voice.

Although he was thirty-four years old, his mother still concerned herself with his developing a socially acceptable relationship. She had made it clear to him that his ideal woman should be from a good family, attractive, and free from any children from a previous marriage. In the last few years, since the end of his short-lived marriage, he had not pleased her with his philandering. He knew it unnerved her that he kept company with women who lacked social breeding. It annoyed her that her son dated women whose IQs were probably no higher than their bust sizes. A professional man like her son had no business risking his reputation or wasting his time on those kinds of women, she often admonished him. She realized that his marriage had been riddled with all kinds of problems and had caused him deep pain. Like any mother who loved her child, she worried over the deep funk he had fallen into after his marriage ended.

However, when his mood had made an upswing to his "Casanova" persona, she had been just as concerned. After all, there was that dreaded virus around! And heaven forbid he should allow a sexy body to make him think he could find lasting happiness.

Oletha Wagner was a snob, he knew—but she was an adorable snob. Though she hadn't been a very affectionate mother to him when he was growing up, he knew that she truly loved him in her own way.

Entering the well-preserved, hundred-year-old house, Addison was again reminded of the many lonely times he had spent there as a child, yearning for his parents' attention. There had been too much loneliness, he remembered. His parents had been young and very much in love with each other. They were always off on some exotic trip with friends, or going to meetings or gala parties or dinners. Addison had always felt like an outsider with Oletha and Cleveland, his father. They seemed only to have eyes for each other, forgetting the little boy who was a product of their love.

"Hello, sweetie," Addison's mother greeted him, appearing in the foyer at the sound of his entrance.

As usual, Oletha Wagner looked marvelous, dressed in a tailored green and black blazer, a black skirt, and a creamy silk blouse. Her diamond-studded earrings peeked from beneath her carefully coiffed brown hair.

"Mother, you're on your way out," he said, noticing that she carried a purse. He leaned over to kiss her. "Sorry. I tried to get here as soon as I could break away from my office, but I had to stop at the hospital to check on a few patients."

"I had hoped you'd come sooner," she said, touching a familiar chord of guilt within him. She studied her delicate gold watch. "I still have time for a visit before I have to be off to my meeting." She took him by the arm and escorted him into the huge living room. "Come sit with me," she ordered, sitting on the mauve Victorian sofa and patting the cushion beside her. "Would you like a drink? Something to eat? I can have Mrs. Overby bring you anything you want."

Addison unzipped his brown leather jacket and shrugged out of it, laying it on the back of a chair. Taking the seat next to his mother, he folded his arms and crossed his legs at the knee, giving her his rapt attention. He sensed that he was in bad favor with her when her glowing expression dimmed to somberness. "Is everything all right, Mother? You seem preoccupied. Worried."

"Things couldn't be better with me. But I'm troubled over your actions, son. I'm hurt that you haven't brought your young woman to meet your father and me—the one you've been spending most of your time with. Imagine how I feel when our friends tell me they've seen the two of you out with some little girl. And I don't have the slightest idea who they're talking about!"

The side of his mouth twitched, then gave way to a wry grin. He didn't want to argue with her over his personal life. "I thought you called me here because you missed me. I didn't expect to be interrogated like a criminal."

She touched his knee and smiled. "Stop being silly. Tell me what is going on with you and this young woman."

A flicker of apprehension coursed through him. His mother wasn't going to approve of Nina, and he knew it. He eased his mouth into a boyish grin, hoping to charm his mother. Trying to appear casual, he stretched out his leg and was about to rest his foot on his mother's prized antique table when she shot him a warning look just the way she used to when he was a boy. He sat forward, disliking the way she still had the power to make him feel like he was a kid.

"Believe me, I'm not trying to keep anything from you," he

lied. "It's just that I've been busy, and so have you and Dad." He rubbed his chin pensively. "I'll start with the basics." He met his mother's intense stare. "Her name is Nina Sterling. Dr. Nina Sterling. She has been practicing in Harper Falls for only a few years. She's an obstetrician and gynecologist. We work together at the free clinic, and we got to know each other better at the hospital and working on various committees. She's bright, and almost as gorgeous as you." He touched his mother's arm, seeking understanding. "And I like her better than I have any woman in a long time."

Oletha stared at her son with interest and trifled with the diamond cluster ring on her right hand. "There is a little girl involved," she said, her voice showing her disapproval. "Is it her child? Is she divorced? A single parent?"

"Take it easy, Mother. That would be Chloe, okay? She's five years old, and she belongs to a childhood friend of Nina's who is having some problems. Nina is only the child's temporary guardian."

She raised a skeptical eyebrow. "What kind of problems would make a professional woman like Dr. Sterling take in another person's child? My goodness, how does she manage such responsibility?"

Her reaction and her comment chafed him. "Well, I won't go into detail over Chloe's problems with you. I think Nina is a good woman to do what she's done with the child."

"I hear you've been playing quite the family man role. I'm told you've been seen in the park on several occasions, scampering with the young woman and the child." There was a critical tone to her voice. "Oh, Addison, I simply can't believe this! With all the fine young women in Harper Falls who would love to be with you, you go and find a woman I've never even heard of! And with someone else's problem child. I certainly hope this relationship is fleeting."

He had considered bringing Nina to meet his parents, but now he was glad he had waited. Telling his mother about Nina was much better than allowing her to make his love interest feel as though she didn't measure up to the Wagner family standards. Of course, he wasn't about to bring up the fact that his mother had gone out of her way to make sure that he married his first wife, Vanessa Kincaid. Vanessa had met all of his mother's social criteria, but that hadn't kept the marriage from being a disaster.

He lifted his chin and stared at his mother boldly. "This isn't a fling, Mother. I'm very serious about Nina."

Oletha pursed her lips. "Who are her people? Was she reared in this area?"

Irked by her aloof manner, he gnawed his lower lip. He certainly didn't want to become disrespectful to her. "She has no one. Her parents are deceased. Both of them died when she was a child. She grew up as a ward of the state. Despite that, she managed to become quite a woman, and quite an admirable person and professional as well."

Oletha's eyes widened with a mixture of surprise and horror. "Oh, my goodness," she said softly.

"Mother, don't look that way," he said with a twinge of annoyance. "You of all people should be proud that your son has found such a good woman. After all, most of those charities you work with are raising money for urban and foster kids, like Nina once was. She's living proof that all your efforts and good work in your civic organizations have paid off—the ones that have kept you so busy through the years. I certainly hope you aren't going to be hypocritical by closing your mind to Nina before you've had a chance to meet her and get to know her."

Mrs. Wagner held her chin higher at her son's belligerent tone. "Don't be rude," she chided impatiently. "It's just that I find it difficult to see what you two can have in common other than your professions and that clinic. You need a woman in your life who is closer to our social circle."

"Vanessa was from our social circle," he said bitterly, "and look what a disaster that turned out to be."

"Well, you two were so young, and too immature to deal with . . . with what happened."

Addison rubbed his hands together, shaken by the memory of Vanessa, then he glowered at his mother. "I don't think about my marriage to Vanessa anymore. It does no good. Right now, I'm with Nina because I want to be. I'm no longer that young man who needs his parents to tell him what is best for him. I'm quite capable of running my life." His frustration crept up his neck like a hot hand. Being this touchy over Nina validated his deep emotions for her even more.

Oletha clutched the delicate gold chains around her neck. "So, will you bring this Dr. Sterling to the annual Community League banquet?" Her voice was tight with tension.

"Yes, I will."

"Good. I want you to be there. I'm going to receive their Humanitarian Award this year." A smile eased the corners of her mouth.

"Congratulations." A glint of satisfaction lighted his eyes. He leaned over to hug his mother. "You're going to have to build another room for all the trophies, plaques, and awards you've received over the years," he said. He felt a momentary pang of regret, thinking of all the activities that she had been recognized for and that had kept her from him when he was growing up and needed to feel her love.

"I'm only carrying out tradition and what I was taught to do," she said. "The Fergusons—my family—and the Wagners have always been committed to our community. You know that, dear." Her bejeweled hand stroked the side of his face. "I'd love to talk longer, but I really have to leave."

He stood and followed her into the front foyer. "No problem. I should be going, too. You'll have your chance to meet Nina soon enough."

"I can hardly wait," she said in a monotone. "Make yourself comfortable," she called over her shoulder as she breezed out the door.

Alone in the big house that had once been his home, he wandered back into the living room. He glanced at the family pictures that were staggered on the elegant mahogany piano. There were framed pictures of generations of Wagners and Fergusons, going back to the end of the Civil War. Proud in stature and impeccably dressed, those relatives had been paragon citizens. The members of his family were all hues, from ebony to near-ivory. They had all been instilled with the need for an education of some kind, so that they could never be enslaved in any form ever again. They had been prosperous farmers, landowners, laundresses, and seamstresses who had reared generations of professionals like doctors, nurses, lawyers, and educators.

As a boy, Addison had often been reminded of his heritage and his responsibility to the Ferguson and Wagner names. And he would tell the children he would have one day of the families' achievements.

If things turned out the way he hoped between him and Nina, their wedding portrait, along with their childrens', would find a place beside the other ancestors on the piano and on the mantel, in this room full of nostalgia.

He frowned. Oletha Wagner was not thrilled that he had chosen someone like Nina as the object of his affection. He had recognized the tight-lipped expression she wore, listening to him speak of Nina. Though he respected his mother, he wasn't going to be intimidated by her. In the past month or so, he had come to love Nina. He wasn't going to allow his mother's shortsightedness to spoil what he believed in his heart was perfect for him at this time in his life.

It would be absolutely ludicrous, he mused, settling on the sofa and propping his feet on his mother's precious table—knowing she would have a fit if she could see him. He slumped down to get comfortable and rested the back of his head on the sofa. He placed his hands on top of his head, closing his eyes in order to conjure up visions of Nina's lovely face and wonderful smile.

"Dr. Wagner," Mrs. Overby called softly. "There's a call for you." She smiled, handing him the portable phone.

"Thank you," he said to the older woman, who was halfway out of the room. He placed the phone to his ear, expecting the call to be from his office.

"Addison, it's Nina." Her voice was weak and tremulous.

"Nina, what's wrong?"

"It's Jenny. She's disappeared. I've had them search the entire nursing home and the grounds to make sure that Earl hasn't been up to his usual crazy antics."

"Stay calm. I'm on my way. It might not be as bad as we think."

By the time Addison made it to the nursing home, he found Nina pacing back and forth in front of the room that belonged to Jenny.

"Okay, what's the deal?" he asked, taking her hand to comfort her.

"The nurse went to give Jenny her medication an hour ago. She had vanished. All the nurse found was the hospital gown on the bed and Jenny's things cleared away." She heaved a sigh of exasperation. "This is Earl's doing. I just know he sweet-talked her into leaving with him to prove to us he still has control over her."

"She was almost better. She should be all right," Addison said, hoping to reassure Nina, even though he hated the situation.

"She'll never be all right with that creature," Nina snapped. "And what about Chloe? She's given no thought at all to her own child. She just up and left."

"Where is Chloe, anyway?" he asked.

"She's with Kimberly and her kids."

"Thank goodness for that. She doesn't need to be in the mess that Earl has masterminded."

"What am I supposed to tell her? How can I explain to her that her mother has disappeared?"

"Let's hope Jenny will contact you later. I can't believe she's not concerned about Chloe."

"I hope you're right," Nina said. "I was talking to Jenny the other day about moving in with me. I thought if she had some time away from Earl, she could make a new life for herself and Chloe. Hopefully, she would see that she doesn't have to take his abuse and that she could survive without him." Nina's eyes darkened with frustration.

"Let's go get Chloe from Kimberly's and take her to your place. We'll have the nursing home call us if they learn anything. Maybe Jenny will call before the day is up." He squeezed her hand. "And maybe you and I can come up with an explanation for Chloe that won't be too difficult for her to understand."

"We have no other choice, do we?" She gazed into his eyes, seeking comfort for her nerves and the crazy turn of events. She held his hand tightly and walked slowly out of the nursing home, thinking about poor Chloe who had been deserted.

Chapter X

After a day of running the prenatal clinic almost alone, Nina was weary and frazzled. When her friend, Kimberly Griffith, appeared for a visit just when the clinic closed, she linked arms with Nina and led her to the clinic's staff lounge.

"You look bushed, girl," Kimberly said, preparing chamomile tea. "What happened to your other volunteers? And where is Addison?"

"He had an emergency at the hospital and then some meeting to attend," Nina explained. She bit into a chocolate chip muffin to ease her hunger pains from missing lunch.

"I like a woman who knows her man's every move. You two are getting nice and cozy. I like that." Kimberly sat beside Nina and helped herself to a piece of her friend's muffin.

"We're all right. He makes me feel . . . feel . . ." Nina's eyes lit up as she searched for an appropriate description. She laughed and felt her face glow.

"Makes you feel like what?" Kimberly's smile matched hers.

"I can't put into words the way he makes me feel."

"Oh, please." Kimberly laughed. "This is really getting too sweet."

"But it's the truth. The feelings are frightening. I find myself thinking about him all the time."

"That isn't something bad—sounds like love to me. It's what you've been needing in your life for a long time."

"I didn't say anything about love, Kimberly. Addison and I enjoy each other's company. But the love word hasn't been mentioned."

"Oh, I see." Kimberly lifted her eyebrows. "I do know that Addison isn't seeing anyone else. So I'm sure it won't be long before you'll hear that four-letter word."

Nina sipped her tea. "And to think I'd given up on men. I figured no man would be interested in ordinary-looking me."

Kimberly grinned. "Are you fishing for compliments? You've come a long way from being ordinary."

"You know I'm not like that."

"Nina, you're gorgeous. In the last few months, I've watched you transform. It didn't happen all at once. When you got rid of those huge glasses, I was impressed. Then all of a sudden you cut your hair and changed the way you dressed. You even sashay when you walk now." Kimberly laughed. "I think that tail-twitching walk of yours is what has Addison mesmerized."

"Only you would come up with something like that." Nina grinned. "I did change, though. I'd been working so long and so hard that I hadn't taken the time to pamper myself. I guess I reached a point in my life where I decided to look out for myself a little better. I think that loving yourself flows over into everything else you do."

"I've been trying to get you to change for years, but you refused. But I'm glad you did. To me you were a beautiful person, but now you're simply fabulous." Kimberly beamed at her friend. "It's a shame you're saddled with Chloe, now that you're in the middle of this romance with Addison."

"I don't look at her that way. She's been a blessing in a lot of ways. She really has." Nina's eyes revealed serenity. "If Chloe hadn't come into my life, I might not have given myself the chance to really know Addison. And you should see the changes she's made in him. It's amazing to see how sensitive and caring he is with her."

"You think he'll make a good father someday?" Kimberly asked, staring at Nina mischievously.

"Yes. He's going to make a fine father." Nina chuckled, knowing what her friend wanted to insinuate.

"Hmm . . . the same way that you'll be a perfect mother."

"Enough, Kimberly. I'm taking one day at a time. Besides, Chloe won't always be with me. Her mother is bound to come to her senses and come get her child any day. Then Addison and I might go back to being at odds with each other, the way we used to."

"I doubt that you can go back to being the way you used to be. You two share a cozy history because of Chloe."

Nina sipped her tea and contemplated what Kimberly had said. There was nothing she'd like better than to have a healthy relationship with Addison. Chloe had allowed them to feel like a family. With Chloe out of the picture, Nina knew that she and Addison would have to learn to deal with each other as a man and a woman, with personal and intimate hurdles to jump.

"I love going to weddings," Kimberly said, leaning toward her and chuckling softly.

"Please, Kimberly, give me a break, will you? With the

chaos that my life is in at the moment, I can't dare to think about something like that."

"Dream, girl. That's what makes everything happen. Can't you just picture yourself married to Addison and having maybe five or six gorgeous children with him? Did you know that he's said he would love to have a large family, because he grew up being an only child?"

"Has he really said that, or are you just putting me on?"

"I wouldn't lie to you. I've heard him myself."

"Enough with the dreams and fantasies. Addison and I are nowhere near talking about marriage." Nina's eyes brightened. "Hey, I forgot to tell you that Addison wants me to attend some high-class affair honoring his mother. She's supposed to be accepting some award for community service."

"I read something in the paper about that. They have this thing every October. Are you going?"

"If I can get you to babysit, I will."

"That's no problem. Chloe is always welcome at my house."

"I knew I could count on you. I'm nervous about meeting his parents for the first time. I wish we could meet in more private circumstances. I'm going to feel like I'm on display. According to Addison, several relatives and friends of the family will be attending."

"Oletha Wagner is a society babe if there ever was one. Wait until you meet her. She is the epitome of class and style. She's done a lot of good things, though." Kimberly finished her piece of muffin. "You have nothing to worry about. As far as I'm concerned, you're in their league. Go and show them what a lucky man Addison is to have someone as special as you in his life."

Though Nina knew Kimberly was trying to boost her confidence, she'd only filled her with more anxiety. She stirred uneasily in her seat. She couldn't imagine being fully accepted by Addison's family. She had no background other than what had been provided by welfare.

She pushed aside her sense of foreboding. "Save time in your schedule tomorrow afternoon," she said. "I'm going to need you to go to the mall with me to find a proper dress. You're used to going to these kinds of functions with your husband, so you know what's appropriate. At least I can look good, even though I'll probably feel out of my element."

"You've come to the right person. I can think of three boutiques to hit right now."

"Please be gentle with me. I don't want you to wear me out in the mall," Nina warned her friend, shaking her head with amusement. She rose from her chair and stretched her tired muscles.

"This is turning into a real Cinderella story. You have the prince, and now you're going to the ball to meet the king and queen—sort of." Kimberly snickered.

Nina smiled. "And let's hope the evening ends happily ever after. Come on, I have to go pick Chloe up from day care. I promised her we would eat at Burger King."

"You've spoiled that kid."

"She's spoiled me with all her laughter and her affection. I'm going to miss her when I have to give her up. I'm so upset with Jenny for walking out on her."

"What could Jenny have been thinking? Has she called recently?"

"Yeah, I talked to her a few days ago. She still wouldn't tell me where she was staying with Earl. All I know is that they're far away from Harper Falls. And he's working and trying to prepare to bring Chloe back to them."

"Why is she being so mysterious?"

"It's that crazy Earl who's controlling her. He's probably afraid that I might try to interfere."

"He needs a good kick in the behind, that's what he needs. What's to love in a confused man like him?"

"Don't ask me. I just don't get it. These women in abusive relationship keep going back for more, believing things will change and that the man will get better with their help." Nina frowned, thinking how duped Jenny had been by Earl. It was only a matter of time before Earl would lose control and harm Jenny again.

* * * * * * * * * * * * *

Arriving at the Black Women's Urban Auxiliary Banquet at the Marriott Hotel, Nina felt her confidence fading fast. She wished she hadn't consented to meeting Addison's parents for the first time under such fishbowl-like circumstances. She felt as though she were on display for their approval. And although she had gone way over her budget with the jade-colored designer dress Kimberly had selected for her, she still felt like she was back in school—the shy, insecure "welfare girl" in hand-me-downs. Oh God, she thought, praying for courage. What am I doing in this crowd?

The affair was peopled with some of the most wealthy and prestigious inhabitants of Harper Falls. The women were dressed in sequined dresses, and genuine diamonds and gold jewelry glittered on their fingers, ears, and necks. The men were distinguished-looking in their tailored suits, with gold watches or bracelets peeking from beneath the cuffs of their shirts. These people belonged to a world that was completely removed from the one she had grown up in, or even lived in today as she struggled to shape her career.

"Nina, relax, baby," Addison said, patting her hand. "You're one of the most stunning women here." He kissed her cheek and smiled at her.

His compliment meant a lot. Still, her heart galloped when he introduced her to a short, stocky man who was a noted criminal judge.

"Pleased to meet you, Dr. Sterling," Judge Delaney said to her. "Addison, you've finally managed to find a young woman with brains and beauty." He gave Addison a knowing wink, then the judge turned his attention back to Nina. "Addison is a fine man. But he and my son, Harold, used to worry me. They were always up to some mischief, pulling pranks on me and his father." He laughed heartily. "Remember that snowy winter you and my son ambushed me with snowballs at my house?"

"Do I ever," Addison said, placing his arm around Nina's shoulders. "But you got even with us when I slept over at your house. You insisted on fixing us one of your favorite sub sandwiches while we watched television." He grinned at Nina. "The judge spiced it up with heavy dashes of hot sauce. Yuk!"

The judge laughed. "I'll never forget the look on your faces. At sixteen, you two were so greedy that you had nearly chowed down half of it before the spice started to burn."

Nina laughed at the good-hearted shenanigans.

"They were good boys. We had plenty of fun together." The judge slapped Addison on the back.

"How is Harold and his family?" Addison asked. "I haven't talked to him in weeks."

"Fine. Great. You know, he and his wife just learned they're expecting their third child."

"Get out of here! That's wonderful," Addison replied with pleasure. "I have to call him to congratulate him. I've got to make plans to visit him in Chicago."

"You do that. And take this pretty lady with you. It was nice meeting you, Nina," Judge Delaney said warming before moving on.

Making their way through the crowd, Nina held Addison's hand tightly, the same way Chloe always held onto hers when they were out and the child was uncomfortable.

Glamorous women came up to Addison to exchange hugs and kisses. They were introduced as childhood friends or acquaintances of his mother and father. He had a smile and a witty exchange for everyone he met. He also made a point of introducing Nina to everyone and including her in the cordial conversations. She felt proud that he made certain everyone knew she was with him; it alleviated some of her tension.

As she and Addison continued through the knot of people to find their table, he was confronted by a red-haired, mahogany-complexioned, drop-dead-beautiful woman. Standing close beside him, Nina could feel his body stiffen.

"There you are, darling," the woman said. "I've been waiting to see you all evening." She hugged him and kissed his face, ignoring Nina's presence. "You look good enough to eat."

"It's nice to see you, Vanessa." He backed away with an odd expression on his face. "How are you?"

"I'm great. I've seen your mother, and we had a nice chat. I was quite honored when the Auxiliary asked me to make the presentation to her. She will always be my favorite mother-in-law."

Nina's brown eyes widened in astonishment at what she had heard. Kim had told her that Addison was married before, but she hadn't expected his ex-wife to be so beautiful—or so possessive, as though there was still something between them.

Vanessa stared at Nina, looking pleased at the way her disclosure had affected Addison's date. "And who is this?" she purred.

"Vanessa, this is Dr. Nina Sterling. Nina, this is Vanessa Wagner." Addison's voice was flat and cold as he said her name.

"Hi there," Vanessa said, feigning enthusiasm. Her glance flickered on and off Nina as though she were an insignificant speck. Then she turned to Addison with a seductive smile. "Oh, sweetie, I've left a smudge of my lipstick on your face." She moved to him and attempted to brush her fingers across his cheek.

"Vanessa, I've got it." He scowled and stepped away from her. He reached inside his jacket pocket for his handkerchief to wipe away the signature of her lips.

"Excuse me. Wifely habits are hard to break," she murmured.

Nina noticed that her smile had become brighter, while Addison appeared to be decidedly uncomfortable.

"I would like to find Mother," Addison said, looking over Vanessa's shoulder.

"Sure. I understand. It was nice meeting you . . . uh, Deena," Vanessa said to Nina. "Darling, we'll talk more later." She toyed with Addison's tie. Then she breezed away through the crowd.

Seizing Nina's hand, Addison squeezed it. "Pay her no mind. I'll explain her later. Just don't go forming any crazy opinions until you hear what I have to tell you."

Hiding her anxiety behind a smile, Nina nodded. That Vanessa person looked as though she still had some claims on Addison and his family. She felt her heart sink. She was not up to competing with this sultry, sophisticated woman who seemed to fit so well into his society world.

She turned to glance in the direction where Vanessa had gone. She saw her in conversation with a matronly woman who seemed to be studying Nina intently. Were they talking about her? Were they saying how shameful it was for Addison to be dating down? All her old fears and demons about not being good enough resurfaced from her past. No matter how successful she became, she could not forget how she had been treated like a pariah because of her indigent and grim background.

"Addison, dear, you had me worried." An elegant woman stepped up to him and took his arm. "I thought you were going to be late. I wanted to be able to introduce my handsome, successful son to all these wonderful people when I make my speech." She gazed up at him with love and pride.

Addison kissed her and draped his arm around her shoulder. "Nina, this is my mother."

Coming face-to-face with the forbidding Oletha Wagner, Nina felt her heart tremble; her mouth became so dry that her throat ached.

"Is this the young lady I've heard so much about?" Mrs. Wagner asked, giving Nina a forced smile.

"Dr. Nina Sterling. One of the best physicians at St. Luke's, and a devoted worker at the free clinic," Addison said. He was clearly trying to ease the hint of anything negative Nina might have suspected from his mother's cool statement. "I'm fascinated as well by the lovely woman she is." He reclaimed Nina's hand and intertwined his fingers with hers, staring pointedly at his mother.

Nina was grateful for his support. She managed a small smile. "Mrs. Wagner, congratulations on your recognition. I'm honored to meet you."

"Thank you, dear," Oletha Wagner responded with an artificial smile. "I'm glad Addison brought you this evening. Maybe we'll have time to talk later." She reached up and patted her son's face. "Addison, you and Nina should find the table I've reserved for you." She pointed to the side of the room. "They're about to begin, and I want you to be prepared to stand, sweetheart." She floated across the room to the head table, leaving behind the heavenly scent of perfume.

Nina exhaled with relief. At least the initial introduction was out of the way.

"She likes you. I can tell," Addison said, squeezing her hand as they walked through the crowd toward their reserved table.

"She is exquisite, Addison," Nina said. She wasn't about to let on that she knew his mother was going to have to get used to her, and vice versa. "She has the grace and style of Lena Horne."

He smiled. "My mother was in the theater for a short while, and she even did some fashion modeling. My father spotted her in a charity fashion show and became obsessed with her." Amusement flickered in the eyes that met hers. "Remind me to tell you about their whirlwind romance. I'm sure you'll love it." He placed his hand at the small of her back and guided her toward their table.

"Get over here, son. I was wondering when you were going to show up," said a man who looked like an older and heavier version of Addison. He rose to his feet. He had black, wavy hair that was streaked with grey, and he wore large, brown-framed glasses.

"I had orders from Mother, so you know I couldn't miss being here." Addison placed his arm around his father's shoulders. "Dad, I'd like you to meet Dr. Nina Sterling. Nina, my father—Cleveland Wagner."

Cleveland Wagner beamed at Nina; his eyes sparkled with delight. "She's a looker, son. One thing I can say about us Wagner men is that we always have good taste in women. Yes, we do." He moved to the back of Nina's chair to pull it from the table for her. "Have a seat, dear. It's a pleasure to have you with us this evening."

Sitting at the table with two other middle-aged couples, Nina exchanged polite hellos and friendly glances. She smiled awkwardly, trying to think of something clever to say until Addison finished chatting with his father and got around to the introductions.

"I'm sorry for talking so long. I haven't seen or spoken to my father for a couple of weeks." Addison settled into the chair beside her, greeting each person with a warm hello. He proceeded to introduce Nina to Reverend and Mrs. Walton, who were known to him as Uncle Casey and Aunt Jessie—his godparents. The other couple was the Neals, Carolyn and Ted. Ted Neal served on the school board with his mother, Addison explained. Unlike the Waltons, who were open and friendly toward Nina, the Neals received her less enthusiastically.

Nina was glad when dinner was served. The attention was taken away from her and placed on other community topics. She still found herself almost too nervous to enjoy the food, though Cleveland Wagner seemed to be doing all he could to make her feel welcome.

With the tinkle of a bell, the moderator for the night's events finally requested the crowd's attention. The formal ceremonies were about to begin.

This portion of the evening turned out to be a long one, filled with speakers who delivered speeches and accolades to Mrs. Oletha Wagner for her contributions and commitments to the community. And then it was time for the guest of honor to speak.

Nina wasn't surprised to see that Oletha was an eloquent speaker who enthralled the group with her charm and words about being responsible to those in need. At the end of her captivating talk, she received a beautiful plaque—presented by Vanessa—that commemorated her as woman of the year. Then the audience rose in a standing ovation.

Nina was uncomfortable with Vanessa playing such an instrumental role in the evening. Was Vanessa still considered a part of Addison's family? she wondered. Her concern about Vanessa waned as she watched Addison staring proudly at his mother and not his ex-wife. His face softened, revealing his love and respect. This tender quality of his endeared him to her even more.

"Mother will be here all night, accepting congratulations and greeting friends," Addison whispered to Nina. "Let's give her our well wishes and get out of here."

Nina felt as though a burden had been lifted from her shoulders. She had met his parents, a few relatives, and some of their friends. She had survived the ordeal.

However, as they made their way across the room through the dispersing crowd, Nina spotted Vanessa at Oletha's side. Vanessa's arm was around Oletha's waist as they posed for pictures. Oletha's smile was genuine; she and Vanessa conversed as though they were quite chummy.

The sight of them aroused Nina's curiosity about this marriage of Addison's. Seeing how close Vanessa and Oletha still were, she wondered if Vanessa and Addison were equally at ease with one another. Perhaps Vanessa had reconciliation on her mind? Nina thought. She knew that some people divorced, only to remarry when they realized they still loved each other. She hesitated as they neared Addison's mother. He turned to look at her, a questioning expression in his eyes.

"You go on and tell her good night," Nina said. "After all, I'm not really family or even a close friend."

He frowned and glanced toward his mother with Vanessa close by her side. His face lit with understanding. "Look, Nina, it's over for me and her. She's nothing more than a family friend." He placed his arm around Nina's waist, pulled her close to his side, and kissed her cheek.

Reassured, she smiled, nodded graciously, and wished Oletha the best.

136

"Thank you, dear," Mrs. Wagner said curtly before Nina could say anything more. She seized Addison by the arm and positioned him on her other side, while Vanessa and Mr. Wagner finished off the group. Oletha ordered the photographer to snap the shot. Nina looked on, crushed by the snub and the woman's indifference to her presence.

After the picture, Addison gave Nina an apologetic look. He kissed his mother good night and returned a cool embrace to Vanessa. She wrapped a graceful arm around his neck, stared into his eyes, and gave him a teasing smile. Frowning, he broke away from her to return to Nina.

"It's no big deal. Really," he told Nina, taking her hand. "I can't wait to get to my place where we can have some privacy. I have some Chardonnay chilling for us. We can take off our shoes, kick back, and relax." His voice was full of promise, and his eyes smoldered with romance.

"I think it would make your mother much happier if you took Vanessa home. It appears that she's the belle of this shindig." Nina spun away from him and marched away. His mother's rejection and Vanessa's blatant flirting had stung her more than she cared to admit.

He caught her by the elbow and firmly escorted her out of the hotel. "Nina, please, don't let their actions come between us. Believe me, neither one of them can influence me any more. I love you. No one can take that from me."

She swiveled slowly to face him, her heart swelling at the unexpected words he'd spoken.

"That's right, I love you," he said. He gave her a smile that set her pulse racing. "I haven't said it before now because you wanted us to slow things down. I've been as patient as I can, waiting for you to give me some kind of sign to let me know you were ready to take our relationship to another level."

Standing outside the hotel in view of the departing guests, Nina had no qualms about kissing Addison. He held her snugly against him. She could feel his heart pounding as hard as hers.

"I love you, too," she said. "I was afraid to let you know, because I didn't want to be hurt anymore."

He gazed at her, then caressed the side of her face. "Angel, I would hurt myself before I'd hurt you." He spoke in a soft tone.

She looped her arm around his to share another tender kiss. She experienced divine ecstasy now that he had confessed his love.

"Let's get out here," he said, breaking their embrace.

"Yeah, let's get out of here." She giggled, feeling vibrant and alive with joy. "I can't wait to get out of these new shoes."

In front of a roaring fire in Addison's living room, they sat on oversized pillows on the floor, sipping wine. The room was mellow, with music playing softly.

"This is the part of the evening I've been looking forward to more than Mother's dinner," he said, resting his shoulder next to hers.

"Surely you enjoyed seeing your mother being honored," she said, sipping and savoring the taste of the smooth wine.

"It was nice, I suppose. However, I grew up attending those kinds of affairs for my mother, my father, or other relatives. The honors are well deserved—but to be honest with you, I get kind of bored with them."

"You should be ashamed of yourself," she chided.

"Aren't I awful?" He laughed. "Don't get me wrong. I do love that woman, despite her taste for glitz and glamour. I admire her style and her classy way of doing things. But when I was a kid, I used to wish that my mother wasn't as glamorous and meticulous over her appearance. I used to want to have a down-to-earth, playground mom—the kind of mom who wore jeans and sweatshirts and wouldn't give a second thought to climbing on the jungle gym or a sliding board with me for the fun of it."

"You are her heart," Nina said softly. "I saw that tonight. Whenever she looked at you, her love and pride for you was in her eyes. Having her and her love is a precious gift. You are fortunate. You don't know how I yearn for my parents' presence and their love." She sighed pensively.

"But you have me. I can love you. Care for you . . ." He set his glass on a nearby table, then took hers. He wrapped an arm around her midriff, ran a gentle hand along the side of her face, and kissed her tenderly.

His lips were warm and demanding. The sensation of his closeness excited her and sent spirals of ecstasy through her. Raising his mouth from hers, he stared at her. His eyes smoldered with desire. "I want you, Nina. My body is aching for you. It's been too long since we've made love." He pressed his face against her cheek; his breath fanned warmly across her sensitive skin. "I have to confess that I wasn't listening to Mother very closely. I was intoxicated by your beauty and the scent of your perfume. All I could think of was how much I wanted to be inside you." He placed a kiss at the base of her neck.

His words of passion sent a shiver up her spine. The thought of him being inside her enflamed her desire. Leaning away from him, she smiled. "Since we know how we feel, there's no need for us to repress our feelings." She fingered the tiny waves at his nape. "You've won my heart and my trust. I *do* love you," she said in a soft, sultry tone.

Jubilantly scooping her into his arms, he lavished her with a torrid, seeking kiss that made her quiver. He embraced her and rocked her in his arms. "I was running out of things to say and do to convince you of how sincere I was."

Tears misted her eyes. "I wasn't trying to be heartless. I wasn't trying to play games." She rested her head on his shoulder. "I had to be sure that *you* weren't playing games any more."

"I deserved the cold shoulder you gave me in the beginning. Now let's make up for lost time."

Resting his forehead against hers, he proceeded to unzip the back of her dress. Then he slid the garment away from her body. The sight of her full breasts, like two ripened globes of sweet fruit, aroused him. He could not resist kissing her cleavage or nuzzling his face on her softness while he unfastened her bra.

Seeing how his glance lingered on her bosom, her feminine core moistened. The moment he touched her breasts and squeezed them ever so gently, her temperature rose to fevered heights. He ran his thumbs across her nipples until they were peaked like rosebuds.

Yearning welling up within her, Nina reclined upon the pillows on the floor. Addison continued his quest with his lips and his hands, making her feel as though she would vaporize with the joy he gave her. The heat of his face and his wet lips, gliding over her breasts, caused her to moan softly. His lips deserted her pouting nipples to claim her quivering lips. He pulled her against the bare flesh of his chest. She'd been so dazed by his magic that she didn't remember when he had removed his shirt. The flesh of his chest upon hers was hot. She groaned softly as he held her and kissed her. Hovering over her and pulling her into his magnetic gaze, he removed the rest of his clothes and hers without losing the power of the hypnotic passion that intensified with each moment, each touch.

The fire burned low, and the music on the sound system had ended. But she didn't need music or warmth from the hearth—she had the warmth from her man's flesh to cocoon and soothe her. No matter how many times she had been with him, she still felt a thrill from the excitement and the pleasure that he delivered to her. His full, throbbing penetration never ceased to electrify and amaze her. Whenever she was away from him, she found herself daydreaming about how sweet it was when their bodies were locked together with the need of their desire and passion.

As he thrust with slow, lush motions, heat burst inside her like little fires. She clung to him, wrapping her legs around him. Moving in a heavenly tempo, she not only gave him her body and heart, but she also surrendered her soul. Encouraged by his tutelage, she had learned to be a tender lover who knew where and how to tease and please him. Her heart felt as if it was glowing from the luscious, sticky web of love they had fallen into, exchanging open-mouthed kisses, searching touches, and all-consuming embraces. Her tenderness turned to a demanding frenzy, wild with unrestrained passion.

Like an erotic athlete, her blood reached its boiling point. She could no longer endure Addison's mind-blowing thrusts and deep kisses. Seeing his handsome face glimmer with perspiration and twisted with their pleasure, she became hotter with desire. Fervently, she writhed against him. She wanted to be with him when he reached the pinnacle of ecstasy. She moaned and rocked him with her spasmodic motions. Hearing him call out her name and groan, she experienced a dizzying uprush of emotion. Their bodies slapped together as if they were seeking carnal vengeance. Her body felt like it was melting into his; she felt his maleness plunging deeper still, ending in a final wild thrust. The joy of her love and admiration for him blazed within her pounding heart and tingling body.

"I've waited all my life to feel the way I do in your arms," he whispered as she lay cozily in his embrace. "The hunter has been captured by the game," he teased. "And I couldn't be happier, because it's exactly what I want," he murmured in a low and sultry voice. "I love you. I love you, Nina Sterling, with all my heart."

Happiness bubbled within her. She caressed his shoulders, allowing her fingers to trail down the biceps of his arms ever so slowly. She planted a gentle kiss at the base of his neck. "I love you, too, but heaven help me." She chuckled wryly.

He raised himself on his elbow and stared at her. "I wish you didn't feel that way. What's wrong with being in love with me?" He fell on the pillow next to her, pulling her body half over his.

"I'm not trying to put you down," she explained. "You're a kind and a good man, but you and I come from two different worlds. Tonight, I saw firsthand the world you come from . . ."

Holding the back of her neck, he pulled her to him and smothered her words with a kiss. His gentle hands journeyed up and down her curvy body.

"You sure know how to silence a woman," she said, catching her breath after his sweet, lingering kiss.

"Don't penalize me for who I am," he chided softly. "You're not being fair. What you're doing to me is worse than what you told me the kids used to do to you when you were in foster care."

She rested her chin on his chest while he ran his fingers through her hair. He had a point, she mused. No one had any control over their background. He loved her for who she was, and she knew she loved him because of the man he was—certainly not because of his wealth or his social standing, though they might be revered by other materialistic, society-climbing women.

"I'm the one guilty of being a snob, aren't I?" she said apologetically. "I'm sorry. I was only trying to protect myself."

"Don't worry about it. Just don't let it become an issue in our relationship." He hugged her and kissed the side of her neck, then worked his way up to her lips in a slow and tantalizing manner.

She was disarmed. Once again, their bodies came together in the rapture of their love.

Chapter XI

Going over the calendar to approximate the date of delivery with a very-soon-to-be teen mother, Nina glanced up to see Addison exit one of the clinic's examination rooms. He stood at the door, scribbling a prescription.

"Dr. Sterling, I need to confer with you in my office once you're done with your patient," he announced, sliding his last patient's chart onto the rack.

"Of course; I'll be there in a moment," she said coolly, as though they were only professional associates.

"I have a feeling that it's not about clinic business," whispered Sue Kerry, the nurse, as she leaned across the counter. "You two might have the others fooled around here, but you can't fool me."

Nina twisted her mouth to the side in a smile. "And I thought we were doing pretty well." She squeezed Sue's arm affectionately.

Heading for Addison's office, she removed the stethoscope

that dangled around her neck and stuffed it into the pocket of her white jacket. She ran her hand through her hair and moistened her lips. It had been a long, busy day—one where she hadn't even had a break to freshen her make-up or leisurely sip a cup of tea.

She knocked at his office door, hoping that no one else was there.

"Come in," he called.

Entering the office, she found him reading from a stack of correspondence on his desk. He met her gaze, and a smile cut his face. The sight of his expression caused a glow to flow through her. She matched his smile with a warmth that was fueled by her heart. "You wanted to see me, doc?" she said, strolling slowly to the front of his desk to feign casualness.

He gave her a boyish grin, rose from his leather chair, and came to sit on the corner of his desk. He reached out to her and swept her into his arms. "I need some healing from Dr. Feelgood," he said, chuckling as he lavished her neck with kisses. He enfolded her soft form more tightly against him and sought her lips and the recesses of her mouth with his probing tongue.

She went limp in his arms and surrendered to his affection. His lips were warm and soft; their sweetness placed erotic images in her mind and made her body prickle with anxious anticipation. Their lovemaking seemed to get better with each encounter; they couldn't stay away from each other. There was nothing she enjoyed more than to be held against his strong, firm body, lost in hot passion. But with Chloe around, it required careful planning on their part to arrange for romantic interludes at the end of their busy days.

"Is Chloe sleeping over at Kimberly's tonight?" he asked in a gentle, enticing tone. He nibbled tantalizingly at her earlobe and rested his cheek on her shoulder.

145

She shivered at his touch. "Yes, she is," she managed to say at last. "She's all excited about it. Kimberly rented her favorite Disney movies." She caressed his face with the back of her hand.

He gazed up at her. "Wonderful. Tonight we can spend an entire night together. I won't have to drag myself out of bed before Chloe gets up." His arms locked behind her hips, holding her flush against his firm manhood.

She shifted against him, loving the heat that radiated through her body from her dewy core. She looped her arms around his neck and peered into his eyes; they reflected the tenderness she felt for him. "Listen to you. You sound like a kid who can't wait to open presents on Christmas morning."

"I can't ever wait for the kind of gifts you always surprise me with." His eyes gleamed with lustful mischief.

She felt a ripple of excitement. "Sounds to me as though you're planning to be very naughty." She smacked his lips with hers as if they were gum drops.

"I intend to be so naughty with you that Santa is going to scratch me off his list forever."

She feigned a shiver. "Oh, I can't wait, bad boy."

Straightening, he pulled her to him again and fitted his mouth over hers, tantalizing her with the tip of his tongue.

The telephone rang. Addison swore impatiently at the interruption and broke their embrace. He snatched the phone off the receiver, though one arm still held Nina firmly against him.

"Yes, Sue," he snapped, frowning. "Nina is in here helping me with a report." He winked at Nina and gave her a wry grin. "She has a call? Sure, she can take it in here."

Giggling, Nina kissed him once more, than took the receiver from him. "Hello. Dr. Sterling." She managed a professional tone, though Addison was layering her neck with feathery kisses.

She tensed as the conversation progressed. Frowning in concern, Addison halted his affectionate kisses and gave her a questioning look. She moved out of his embrace and scowled.

"Yes . . . yes, thanks for the call," she murmured. "I'll . . . I'll be right there. Just don't let them leave until I get there." She hung up the phone. She felt flushed; she pressed her hands to her face.

"What is it, sweetheart? What's wrong? Tell me," Addison urged, comforting her with an embrace.

She lifted her head slowly to meet his eyes. She stared at him as though she hadn't absorbed what he was saying. She sighed loudly. "It's Jenny. That was Mrs. Richardson calling to tell me Jenny's at the day care to pick up Chloe and take her home."

His expression turned somber. He rested his face next to hers and held her in silence. Clearly, the unexpected news had unnerved him as well. "Is that bum, Earl, with her?"

"I . . . I have no idea. All I know is that Mrs. Richardson said Chloe's mother showed up and insisted on seeing her. Then she announced that she was taking her home. The only thing that kept Jenny from walking out with her was the fact that today is fingerpainting day, and Chloe refused to leave until she had done her artwork. You know how much she loves that stuff." Nina managed a smile. She was grateful that Chloe had been stubborn today. It gave her time to get over there.

"I've got to go," she said. "Now. I can't just let Jenny leave without having the courtesy of letting me know what her plans are. I deserve better than this," she fumed. "I've got to get over there. Earl is obviously behind her sudden appearance. He must be making plans for Jenny to get on welfare with Chloe. I guess he's out to show me how much power he can wield over his woman." She whirled around and headed for the door.

"There's nothing you can do to keep her from taking her own child. You were supposed to be the guardian only until she was able to care for her again." Addison held onto her wrists to keep her from fleeing.

Tears welled in her eyes. It hurt to think of Chloe going back into the same grim situation as before. In the last few months, she had become accustomed to the child's lively presence. She had enjoyed her curiosity and hunger for learning. She had come to love Chloe almost as much as she loved Addison. The three of them were like a family. The thought of having her ripped out of her life so rudely made her heart ache.

She broke from Addison's grip. "If Jenny doesn't seem emotionally capable, I'll . . . I'll report her . . . to . . . child . . . child protective services. I won't have her taking that little girl into her mess of a life. I won't! It breaks my heart the way Chloe still awakens from nightmares about Earl and his cruelty to her mother."

She was almost out the door when he called to her, "Wait for me! I can't let you face this alone. Remember, I care about that girl as much as you do. Surely we can reason with Jenny not to take her. We'll bargain with her, or do whatever it takes to keep Chloe near, so we can watch over her." He grabbed his jacket and followed Nina.

Seeing how upset she was, he insisted on driving her to the day care center. On the ride there, she struggled with her emotions, trying to remain rational and calm. She wanted to wring Jenny's neck for the way she had deserted her and Chloe and for the sneaky way she had slipped into town without notifying her of her plans. She wished she had never given Jenny the name of the day care center and told her its location the last time she had spoken to her. But then she realized it was information due Chloe's mother. Knowing the uncertainty and the stress Jenny was under trying to live with Earl, she believed details of Chloe's day-to-day progress would encourage her and give her the hope she needed to resume her responsibilities.

Now that the time had come for Chloe to be returned to her mother, Nina wondered how she was going to live with the void that would be left by her going. With her childish innocence and candid observations, Chloe had taught Nina how to appreciate the simple things in life. She had shown Nina that she could not avoid the challenges of life or relationships by hiding behind her career the way she had.

When Nina's life had been the bleakest, she had been fueled by her dreams of becoming a doctor. It was a dream she had been fortunate enough to share with her mother before she died. She had made the dream a reality. And she knew that her mother and father in paradise were bursting with pride over her success. But it wasn't enough to have a dream or a wonderful career unless you could share it with someone. Chloe had taught her that.

And most importantly, Chloe's presence had made it possible for her to see that Addison was the best man for her. She didn't want to take Chloe's mother's place. Her only desire was to have Chloe around, so that the little girl could have the love and support a child needed. She still feared that Jenny wasn't strong enough to surround Chloe with the kind of happiness and vision that were required to raise a child. Jenny was still trying to be what a mixed-up Earl wanted her to be. Out of her need for his twisted kind of love, she had made him and his needs her priority in life, instead of placing her attention on Chloe.

No one knew better than Nina how important it was to have love and support and to know that there was someone in your life cheering you on, whether times were good or bad.

Addison reached across the car seat and grasped her hand, breaking her reverie. "Everything is going to work out," he assured her.

She covered his hand and smiled weakly. "I hope so. I really hope so."

"I've been watching you since we've been riding. What's making those brown eyes so blue?"

She hesitated. She had given him very few details about her childhood. But today the memories she ordinarily repressed or smothered by throwing herself into her work flooded her mind and choked her with emotion. She was rocked to the core at the impending threat of giving up Chloe and not ever seeing her again.

"I was thinking about Jenny and me. Jenny was a little older than Chloe when she arrived with the foster family with whom I'd been placed at fourteen. The first day she was brought to that house, she was so scared that she didn't utter a sound the whole day. Once the social worker left her behind, the lady who was our caregiver did nothing to make her comfortable. She told her she didn't have time to pamper anyone and left her alone, huddled on a chair with tears of confusion streaming down her face. By this time, I was an old hand at the system and the insensitive people who were part of it. Being familiar with that feeling of being unwanted and lonely, I made it my business to make Jenny feel welcome."

Addison reached over and touched her knee briefly; his eyes were soft with sympathy.

"As a child, Jenny had lovely, thick hair," Nina went on, turning slightly to look at him. "I remember brushing and combing it, and braiding it neatly while I talked to her about school and told her silly jokes and nursery rhymes the way my mother had taught me at her age. From that day on, I couldn't take a step without Jenny following me. Whenever she wanted or needed anything, she would come to me instead of our cold foster mother. I helped her with her homework, I kept her from getting punished when she got on the woman's nerves with her vibrancy, and I made sure that none of the neighborhood kids picked on her."

"That explains everything," Addison said. "It's clear to me why you so readily took in Chloe for Jenny. You and she were like sisters. I always believed that you two shared a friendship when you were girls. I had no idea of the kind of bond that was between you two. That must have been rough. How in the world did you manage to survive?" Addison's voice reflected compassion.

"Looking back, I often wonder how I made it myself. I did my best for Jenny in those days. Then things got too crazy for me. This woman we lived with, Mrs. Fletcher, acted as though I was a servant. She'd lie around all day, talking on the phone or watching soaps, and expected me to do the cleaning, the laundry, and the cooking for her and her family. She used to criticize whatever I did and call me horrible names. Although I cooked for her and her family, she would never let me or the other foster kids eat the same meals. She used to feed us food that wasn't fresh. It was "their" food and "the foster chilluns" food, which was usually of lesser quality. She was relentless in giving me so many chores that I could barely have time to study. So I started rebelling by refusing to do her work and by speaking up for myself and the other kids she was paid to care for. Mrs. Fletcher didn't like it and accused me of being a troublemaker. She used to slap me around and tried to make me stay in my room. That was when I started slipping out my bedroom window. I'd hang out in the streets and make friends with kids in the neighborhood who had problems similar to mine."

Addison furrowed his brow. "I can't believe that about you. Seeing how professional and conservative you are, I never would have imagined you'd been through such things."

"I tried to be tough, but I wasn't any good at it. I never bothered anyone until they bothered me. I'd put up a good fight to protect my dignity. And I got into my share of trouble with the law, too—shoplifting for feminine things I needed but didn't have the money for. And once I was caught spray-painting obscenities on buildings. I developed an attitude worse than some of the teen girls who frequent the free clinic. However, I consider myself one of the lucky ones who woke up before it was too late."

"What changed things for you? What turned it all around?" Addison's voice was soft and filled with caring.

"One teacher showed interest in me during a period when no one had the time or concern to see my pain. She made all the difference in the world to me. She talked to me and listened to me. I told her what my mother wanted for me, but I thought it was impossible all on my own. She helped me set goals and work to reach them. She saved my life. There's no telling where I may have wound up if it hadn't been for her. Maybe that's why I care so strongly about Jenny. She wasn't as lucky as I was."

By the time she had finished sharing her experiences, they were pulling up in front of the day care center. Nina burst from the car and rushed up the sidewalk and into the school. It was busy with the activity and chatter of preschoolers.

She went straight to Chloe's class and peeked in the small glass on the door. She was relieved to find the little girl still there, working intensely at her fingerpainting. Comforted by the sight of the child, the pace of Nina's heart slowed as she made her way to the office. There she found Jenny, sitting and nervously rubbing her hands together. Her eyes were hidden by sunglasses.

Mrs. Richardson came to greet Nina as she entered the office and pulled her aside to talk privately.

"I appreciate your calling me," Nina told her.

"I'm glad you came right away, Dr. Sterling. I'm glad you made me aware of Chloe's situation the way you did. I wanted to make sure everything was cleared with you before I handed Chloe over to her mother." She nodded in Jenny's direction. "She almost got away with her, but Chloe knew today was finger-painting day. And nothing—absolutely nothing—keeps her from that!" Mrs. Robinson smiled and walked away from the office.

Nina approached Jenny, trying to figure out what her state of mind was. She sat beside her friend.

Jenny folded her arms across her chest and stared at Nina defensively. "I see that woman couldn't wait to let you know I was here for my baby. She *is* my daughter."

"You sure haven't acted like it in the last few months. You made a few phone calls and some big promises to her, but you left me to make excuses for you when you didn't come through like you promised."

"I'm doing the best I can, okay? I've been trying to get straight. Earl and I have been working wherever and whenever we can to make ends meet, and to prepare a home for us with Chloe." Her lips quivered.

"That's good. That's fine," Nina said. "But why were you slipping into town to get Chloe without my knowing? I believe I'm owed more than that. How do you think I would have felt, coming here to pick her up and finding her gone with you? Didn't you care about me at all?" Nina threw her arms wide in exasperation.

Jenny looked away from her disgruntled friend." I . . . I would have called you. Earl gave me the car for a couple of hours. He told me if I wanted Chloe I'd better come now, or else we wouldn't have the chance before we moved on."

"Moved on? Where is he dragging you this time?"

"He's heard there's work in another city. The pay is supposed to be double what he's been pulling in now."

Nina wanted to grab Jenny and shake some sense into her. Couldn't she see that Earl, with his addictions and other emotional problems, was never going to amount to anything, no matter where he lived? "You just told me you were working to prepare a home, and now you're telling me you're getting ready to move to another town. Which is true?"

"Listen, I plan to repay you for all you've done for Chloe. I appreciate everything, I really do—but I need my baby with me. When you're a mother, you'll understand what I mean."

Listening to her, Nina was torn by conflicting emotions of pity and frustration. "I'm not trying to keep her from you. I just want to make sure that everything . . . that everything is safe for her."

Tears slid down from beneath Jenny's sunglasses.

Nina reached out and removed the glasses. She grimaced at the black and blue bruises she saw around Jenny's eyes. "You can't possibly be thinking of taking Chloe back," she said, angrily pointing at Jenny's face.

Jenny snatched her sunglasses back and placed them on her face like a mask. "This has nothing to do with me taking Chloe." Her voice quivered. "He . . . he wants her back with us. That's why I'm here. I can get benefits for Chloe. Money that'll tide us over." She cleared her throat. "Don't make this any harder for me." Her voice came out in a whine. "He's not going to hurt her. She'll make things better. She'll be his inspiration to work for something for us." Jenny tried to force a smile, but it crumbled with her anxiety.

Nina had a sinking feeling in her stomach. What could she do or say to make Jenny realize that things weren't going to get any better as long as she stayed with Earl?

Jenny bounded from her seat. "I have to be getting back. I'm going to get Chloe. She ought to be done with that painting mess by now."

Nina jumped to her feet, stalling for time to bargain with her. "Chloe has a lot of new things I bought her. She has some toys. You can't leave without them."

"I don't have time for all that, Nina. We're going on. Chloe has things Earl and I have been buying for her, too. They might not be as fancy, but they'll do."

"Jenny, please stay overnight. Let's talk about this to see if it's the best thing."

"No, girl, I can't do that. I've made up my mind. If I'm not back soon, my man is going to come looking for us. I don't want any more trouble for me or you. You know that he knows where you live and all."

Chloe came rushing down the hall to her mother when the teacher released the children for recess.

"There's my baby!" Jenny exclaimed, greeting Chloe with open arms and a broad grin that looked forced.

Chloe clung to her mother. She gazed up at Nina. "See, I told you she was coming back soon," she said. "Mama is going to take me to a new house and a new school, Aunt Nina."

Nina knelt to be at eye level with Chloe. "Chloe, you've made so many new friends here. I don't know what we're going to do without you." She gulped back a sudden rush of emotion. She wanted Chloe to say that she didn't want to leave and that she wanted to stay a little longer, giving her mother time to think through her situation.

Chloe turned to Nina and hugged her tightly. "I'll be back to see you and my friends. Mama promised me I could come back. She said that was why I should leave my new clothes and toys with you."

Nina looked at Jenny, feeling as though she'd been stabbed in the back. Her old friend had been clever enough to cover herself for taking the child away without seeing Nina.

Jenny's face held a hint of defiance. "That's right, Nina. We'll be back as soon as we get things lined up where we're going."

"See, I told you," the little girl said, grinning.

"Yes, you told me, sweetheart," Nina said, pulling Chloe to her. She closed her eyes and prayed that God would watch over her and keep her safe from harm. The trusting child had no idea what was waiting for her. She honestly believed there was a new, perfect life ahead.

"Hey, if you're giving out hugs, I want one too." Addison walked into the office and stood near Nina and Chloe.

Chloe broke away from Nina and reached up to Addison. He lifted her into his arms.

A surge of sadness engulfed Nina, but she tried to maintain her composure. She didn't want Chloe to feel any of her anxiety. Maybe this time things would be better for Jenny, she thought. Who was she to judge or stand in her way?

"You be good," Addison told Chloe. "If you ever need your Aunt Nina or me, or just want to talk, you call. Remember how you learned your Aunt Nina's phone numbers and mine, and how I taught you to use the telephone?"

Chloe nodded with a big grin.

Jenny kept her distance while Addison talked to her daughter. "Chloe, we have to go," she said finally. "We have a long drive ahead of us."

Addison set the little girl on the floor, and she rushed to her mother's side.

Nina went to Jenny, took her hand and squeezed it. She was unable to speak. Her nerves were stretched taut. She felt as though a piece had been taken from her heart.

"Thanks . . . thanks for everything." Jenny's voice was low and strained.

"Thank you. She's a joy. Just take care of my little angel," Nina said. "And please keep in touch."

"We will. We will," Jenny said, walking away, holding onto Chloe's hand.

Seeing Nina's face crumple, Addison draped his arm around her shoulders. Once Jenny and Chloe were out of sight, Nina retreated to his embrace and sobbed softly.

Chapter XII

It was a cloudless summer day—one that couldn't have been more perfect for sunning and romping at the beach.

Chloe was dressed in a neon-green bathing suit. She was fascinated by the small village she was creating in the sand, using her red plastic bucket.

Nearby, Nina and Addison watched her. They lay on a blanket side by side, sharing an intimate conversation and affectionate kisses.

When Chloe was bored playing in the sand, she began walking along the shore, searching for seashells.

Nina watched her as she tossed her treasures into her sand pail. However, Addison's charm distracted Nina. She was lost in his smoldering eyes and enchanted by his words of endearment. He emphasized his tender emotions by giving her a lingering kiss that made her close her eyes to savor its sweetness. She forgot everything, even Chloe, for the brief moment of pleasure.

Opening her eyes and catching her breath, she saw no sign of Chloe. She shoved herself away from Addison and jumped to her feet. Panic welled up in her throat. She ran in the direction where she had seen Chloe headed on her seashell hunt, but there was no sign of the child. Then she spotted the red pail. Lying on its side in the sand near the surf was Chloe's sand bucket, shells spilling from it.

"Chloe! Chloe!" She ran and called so loudly that her throat hurt.

"I'll look over here in the bushes. Maybe she's hiding from us," Addison said, dashing away from Nina. He too began frantically calling for Chloe.

Nina stared out at the ocean and gasped at the sight. She saw a tiny form floating on the foamy waves. She rushed out into the water, swimming frantically toward the body. The closer she got, the farther away it drifted. Her arms grew tired and heavy, but she refused to leave the water. She had to get to Chloe. Suddenly, it was difficult for her ot breathe. Every stroke she took felt as if it would be her last one. She sputtered for breath, feeling the pull of the ocean as it overcame her . . .

Abruptly, Nina disentangled herself from Addison's embrace and sat up in bed, breathing hard. She was drenched in perspiration.

Addison, asleep beside her, awakened with a start. He turned on the light. "What is it, baby? Are you okay?" he asked, massaging her shoulders.

"I had an awful dream. It was horrible, and it seemed so real."

"Chloe?" It had been more than two weeks since Chloe's mother had come and taken her away.

She fell back on the pillow and covered her eyes with her hands, trying to get the image of the nightmare out of her mind. Was it a bad omen? Was Chloe safe? she wondered.

Hovering over her, Addison frowned and wiped away the perspiration on her face. "You want to talk about it?"

Nina shook her head. She thought it was better not to mention the horrible dream. She was afraid that if she spoke about it, something awful would actually happen to Chloe.

"You've got to let this thing go," he said, "before it eats you up. We need to have faith that Jenny's love for her will protect her."

She took his hand and lifted it, then kissed his palm. "I suppose you're right. I am being ridiculous, worrying. Chloe is with her mother, and she's safe," she said, hoping to convince herself.

"She's safe, and you're safe and warm with me." He leaned over her. He slipped his hand beneath her nightshirt, seeking the lushness of her inner thighs.

She rolled toward his touch. She undulated sensuously from the warm, seeking wanderings of his hands over her body. He stroked the curve of her waist and hips. She took hold of his proud, firm sheath and caressed its throbbing length. While she worked her magic, he paused. His face eased into an expression of awe and delight. When her hand fell away, he swooped her to him, smothering her with kisses.

She clung to him as he lured her with an open-mouthed kiss that made her mouth ache. Her heated breath mingled with his, electrifying her. He nibbled her lips, then traced her swollen lips with the tip of his tongue, sliding it in and out of her mouth and thrilling her from head to toe.

Leaning away from her, he tugged her nightshirt over her head to expose her nakedness. He fell upon her breasts and nuzzled his face between her mounds. He scooped them in his palms and fondled them gently, brushing his thumbs across the nipples as if they were delicate rosebuds.

Rolling her head from side to side, Nina moaned softly. A delicious fire brewed in her core, and only Addison could quench the desire he had enflamed.

"You look just like an angel," he whispered in awe. He tasted her lips while his hand ran over her body as though he was tracking the course of a wonderful journey. He lingered at her breasts, cupping them and massaging them as his arousal pulsated against her thigh. He wandered to her flat tummy and stroked it while they shared a plundering, hot kiss. Feeling his hand upon her passion flower, she gasped with delight. His fingers probed her soft triangle, sending shivers up her spine, then dipped into her sweet, dewy haven to intensify her pleasure.

Her head fell back and she groaned, relishing the magic he conjured up so magnificently. She felt herself on the edge of satisfaction, until he halted his sweet act to move between her thighs. He placed his hardened member inside her and lifted her bottom to pull her flush against him. He rocked her in the rapturous rhythm of lovemaking. His strokes were slow and steady. She relished the thrill of his hot, potent manhood buried within her. She fell into a wondrous, rhythmic tempo, purring with utter bliss.

In the months since they had been sleeping together, she believed she had experienced all that she was supposed to as a woman. Yet on this night, and at this moment, she was learning another level of sensuality. Feeling beautiful and enchanted, she murmured his name as if it were a prayer. Her body glowed with his every kiss, every touch, every golden thrust. Her heart felt as though it would burst with the raw passion that seeped through her being as their bodies massaged each other.

Suddenly, he began to stroke her with a fierce, desperate urgency. He ran his fingers through her hair until he could grip the back of her neck. With smoldering passion, he gazed down into her eyes.

Feeling his body trembling and releasing the wine of his love, she closed her eyes and gnawed her bottom lip to fully enjoy the shuddering climax that washed over her. She unleashed an uninhibited cry of joy, giving voice to the glory of love they shared. In the afterglow, they cuddled and fell into a deep lovers' sleep.

The next morning, she arose before Addison and hustled to his kitchen to prepare coffee.

He soon appeared, grinning broadly, dressed in faded jeans and a multicolored shirt of red and green that enhanced the glow of his caramel complexion. He rushed up to her and wrapped his arms around her, then kissed her tenderly. His large hand took her face and held it gently while his mouth warmed her with a devastating smile.

"Are you cooking me a ham and cheese omelette?" he asked, staring into her eyes with a wry grin.

"Now, you know I'm not into cooking," she said, leaning toward the counter without breaking his embrace to seize a new box of cereal. "Here," she said, shoving it at him and wiggling out of the circle of his arms. "I'll get the bowls and the milk."

"I love cereal. I love you. A woman as fine as you doesn't need to know how to cook." He laughed, taking a seat and opening a box of raisin bran.

During breakfast, Nina noticed that he was distracted while she talked with him. She had to repeat or explain whatever she said to him. "I guess I've worn out my welcome," she said. His sudden distance awakened her old fears and uncertainties.

"Of course not," he said. "What makes you say a thing like that?"

Ever since Chloe's leaving, her composure had become a fragile shell. "Hmm . . . it's time for me to start acting like a big girl. I need to get back to my house and set things in order. I'm going to box up all the stuff that belonged to Chloe and put it in my attic. You need your space and your privacy. I can't keep avoiding the memories at my place. That's not me. I don't know what I could be thinking, staying over with you longer than I should have."

"There's nothing I like better than going to sleep with you in my arms and still finding you at my side in the morning." He reached across the table to seize her hands in his. He stared at her intently. "I was considering asking you to make it a permanent thing. You know, live with me."

She was too startled by his suggestion to respond. She merely stared, tongue-tied. Yes, she did love Addison, but she didn't know if she was emotionally ready for a live-in relationship. Then, too, she had to consider her reputation. Would she lose the respect of those whom she had worked so hard to impress with her professionalism as a physician? And what about her teenage female patients, who looked up to her and respected her advice about premarital sex and practicing sexual abstinence? What kind of example would she be to them if she openly lived with Addison?

"Addison, I couldn't live with you. It's best that we continue the way we are by living apart, because . . ."

"Would you marry me, then?" he asked matter-of-factly, responding as though he had not heard a word she said.

A wave of happiness washed through her. A tiny smile eased the corners of her mouth. She wanted to hear the question again, to make sure that she had heard him correctly. She cupped an ear. "Excuse me?"

"Will you marry me, Nina?" He spoke slowly and clearly.

"You're serious, aren't you?"

"I wouldn't ask you if I didn't mean it."

"Uh . . . you want an answer now?" she asked, feeling a warm flush on the back of her neck from this unexpected proposal.

"Yes, I do. I know I love you, and you say your feelings are the same for me." He studied her.

Her happiness turned to pessimism. She remembered his mother's reaction to her when they had been introduced. "Your mother doesn't like me. She's not going to . . ."

"I'm a grown man, and my mother doesn't run my life." He shifted in his seat and stretched out his leg, reaching into his pants pocket. He produced a small, red velvet box and opened it, then set it in front of her.

The solitaire pear-shaped diamond was the most lovely piece of jewelry Nina had ever seen. Tears misted her eyes, knowing he had chosen it for her.

"Do you like it? It's as classy and beautiful as you." His voice was soft and sexy. "Won't you please be my wife?"

Moving from her seat, she floated toward him. He welcomed her with open arms and pulled her onto his lap.

"Well, does this mean yes?" he asked, lavishing kisses on her neck.

"Yes. Yes, I'll marry you." She laughed, with tears of joy streaming down her face.

Lifting the velvet box off the table, he removed the diamond from its cushioned bed. He slipped it onto her quivering hand and kissed it. "I love you. I intend to make you happy as long as you will allow me," he whispered. His eyes smoldered with love and devotion.

Her heart thrilled at his words. She wanted this marriage as much as he did, she realized. Now that she had found love with a man as wonderful as he, there was no need for her to let this opportunity pass her by. How many chances did one get to have such a romantic fantasy come true?

"I don't want a long engagement," Addison said with enthusiasm, holding her tightly. "I want us to get married soon, so we can begin our lives. Our family."

"I couldn't agree more." She looped her arms around his neck. The heaviness in her heart was lifted, and she laughed. She was so completely happy. Her gaze locked with his, and her eyes shined as brightly as the sparkling diamond she wore.

* * * * * * * * * * * * * *

When Kimberly learned that Nina and Addison had become engaged, she was as excited as Nina was. She insisted on having the wedding at her home and helping Nina with all the arrangements.

"He wants to go to the Islands for our honeymoon. Montego Bay," Nina told Kimberly while they sat in Kimberly's living room, listening to music and nibbling from a bowl of microwave popcorn. "I used to dream about going to places like that. I never imagined that I would actually be going there as a bride."

"It will be a trip you'll never forget. The place is a heavenly paradise. Perfect for two people in love," Kimberly said, bubbling with excitement. "Oh, Nina, I'm so happy for you!"

"I'm so happy that it scares me. I keep feeling as though I might wake up to discover that this is all a dream."

"It's no dream. All you have to do is to look at that ring on your finger." Kimberly took her hand to admire the ring for the umpteenth time.

"You know what would really make my wedding special?"
"What's that?"

"I wish Chloe could be my flower girl," Nina said wistfully. "She would be so happy to know that Addison and I are getting married. She would love getting all dressed up, with ribbons in her hair."

"She would have gotten a kick out of it. It's so sad that her mother didn't think enough of you to keep in touch." Kimberly's tone of voice made it clear that she thought very little of Jenny for the way she had breezed into town and walked away with Chloe, without any regard for Nina's feelings.

"I only wish them well," Nina said, trying not to think about how much she missed Chloe or how insensitive Jenny had been to her. But those thoughts were for another day. Today she had a different problem. "Addison and I are visiting his parents' home later today. He told me his mother is trying to lay a guilt trip on him, because he didn't tell her about our plans before now."

"I bet Oletha Wagner is beside herself over her grown son getting married without it being sanctioned by her."

"I haven't seen her since the night of the banquet. She was very cool toward me. I got the impression that she was trying to get Addison to notice his ex-wife. She kept pulling Vanessa into pictures with her and Addison, as though she was still part of the family."

"Vanessa is the least of your worries—the tramp. What was between them is over. I'm sure he told you about her."

"He sure did. She was some nightmare for him, even though Oletha seems to adore her. What's with those two, anyway? I mean, if Vanessa had mistreated my son, I certainly wouldn't want to be bothered with her. She's the reason he was turned off by romance and love for years. That's why he started dating around and getting his reputation as a womanizer," Nina said.

"You can't allow his mother or the idea of Vanessa hovering

around the family to spoil the happiness you have. The most important thing is that he wants you."

Nina sighed softly and fingered the stone pensively. "He does make me happy, Kim. He's always been there for me. Even before I really wanted him to be."

"Sure sounds like love to me," Kimberly agreed. "I'm so glad you two are having Thanksgiving dinner with us."

"So am I. Thank goodness his parents will be out of town with some of their close friends. I don't think it would have been a pleasant holiday for me, having to withstand Oletha's aloofness."

"She'll come around. She just needs time," Kim said.

"I suppose you're right," Nina said. She heaved a sigh. "So do you think we can pull this wedding together for the first Saturday in December?"

"I know we can. The key is organization," Kim said, placing a spiral notebook on her lap and poising her pen to write.

"Addison and I don't want to waste any more time than we already have. I told him how I've often dreaded the holidays after my mother died. Thanksgiving and Christmas have always been hard for me. It was his idea for us to get married after Thanksgiving and before Christmas. We'll be able to celebrate Christmas as Mr. and Mrs. Wagner. From here on, he wants me to associate the holidays with our happiness and joy as a couple."

"You've really turned that man around. Who'd ever have thought he would become such a darling?"

"Isn't he wonderful?" Nina smiled, with tears sparkling in her eyes.

"It sure is," Kimberly said. "We'll make out lists of things to do. You take care of things on your list, and I'll certainly take care of mine. Have you been looking around for dresses or a gown yet?"

"No, I haven't. Not with the busy schedule I've had. It seems that all my patients are having their babies at the same time. It's like a baby boom."

"You're going to have to make time if we're going to have you become Mrs. Addison Wagner." Kimberly tapped her pen on the notebook.

Nina touched Kimberly on the arm. "I love having you as my matron of honor."

"I'm so glad you asked me," Kimberly said, opening the notebook. "Let's start with the flowers."

Chapter XIII

On the way to the Wagner house a few hours later, Nina was more nervous about confronting Oletha Wagner than she had been the first time. She glanced uneasily at Addison in the car beside her. She hoped that Oletha wasn't going to make him choose between the two of them. She knew he loved his mother, but he had convinced Nina that he wanted to spend his life with her, regardless of his mother's opinion.

The Wagner's house, a fabulous two-story brick with well-polished windows, took up enough acreage for two spacious homes.

Once inside the house, Nina felt as though she was visiting one of those luxurious homes of the rich and famous she'd often seen in *Ebony*. They were greeted at the door by a friendly faced, middle-aged woman—Mrs. Overby, the housekeeper, Addison told her. She took their coats and told Addison that his parents were in the den upstairs.

Ascending the stairs, Nina scanned the family pictures that

hung along the wall. There were framed pictures of various shapes and sizes, of people from various eras. Their styles of dress and the tint on the old pictures—even their expressions, from somber and dignified to carefree and glamorous—gave a hint of the decade. Nina was fascinated. She had nothing but a few snapshots of her mother and father and herself. That was all. There were no grandparents, and no aunts or uncles or cousins that she knew of. Her parents had both been only children who had lost the few relatives they had. They had grown up in a rural area and relocated to Harper Falls for better opportunities, leaving behind the few friends they had.

Entering the cozy den, Nina and Addison found Oletha and Cleveland watching the cable news channel on their large-screen television. Oletha lounged on the sofa in a satiny lavender pants outfit. Her jeweled fingers worked on an intricate design in needlepoint. At their arrival, she peered over the rim of the reading glasses that were perched on the bridge of her nose.

"Addison. Hello, dear." She smiled broadly at her son and beckoned him to come to her. "Give me my usual kiss."

"Nina, it's nice to see you again," Cleveland Wagner said, rising from his seat to embrace her warmly.

"Nina." Oletha addressed her with a cool smile. "Come over here and sit with me. Let me see that ring my son has given you."

Nina obliged Mrs. Wagner with a smile, though the request made her heart beat erratically.

Knowing how uneasy she was about the evening, Addison sat nearby on the arm of the sofa. When Nina held up her left hand for the inspection, he placed his hand under hers.

Oletha studied the ring, then swung her gaze to Addison. "This is the ring that belonged to your father's mother," she said. She could not hide her surprise or disapproval.

Cleveland strolled across the room and held out his hand to

take Nina's. His smile was warm and welcoming. "Lovely," he said. "The jeweler did a good job of polishing and cleaning it up. It looks like new. My old man had good taste, didn't he?" He and his son shared a knowing look.

Oletha shot her husband an accusing glance. "You did this without even discussing it with me, Cleveland."

"It was a father and son thing, dear." Cleveland slapped Addison on the back. "He had spoken to me about his feelings and his intentions with this young lady. I suggested the ring. It's a shame to have it just lying in the safe deposit box. His grandmother would have loved knowing that Addison gave it to his soon-to-be wife. You know she thought the world of this boy, Oletha."

Nina had had no idea that the ring was an heirloom. From the look on Oletha's face, she didn't know whether to show that she was flattered, or to feel guilty for the treasure and keepsake that adorned her hand.

"I always did love that ring," Oletha said, eyeing the stone. She gave Nina the impression that she didn't consider her worthy of it, even though her husband had made it clear he accepted his son's choice of a bride.

During dinner, Addison and Nina related their simple wedding plans to his parents. Oletha remained quiet while Nina spoke of the small, intimate service they planned to have at their best friends' house, Doug and Kimberly Griffith.

"But, Addison," said his mother, "there are so many family members who will be insulted if you don't invite them. What am I supposed to say when they learn you married without them being there to help you celebrate?"

"Mother, *I* don't have to answer to them. If they care so much for me, their good wishes will be enough."

Oletha pursed her lips and gave her son a disapproving stare. "I wish you would reconsider. You could have a lovely candlelight service in the chapel of the Episcopalian church you were raised in."

"Oletha, it's the bride who plans the service." Cleveland chided his wife. "Not everyone goes for those big shows like Vanessa did." Cleveland caught Addison's eye and cleared his throat. He clearly regretted mentioning his son's ex-wife. "Anyway, if Nina and Addison prefer a small ceremony, so be it. They are adults, and they certainly don't need us to tell them what to do." He winked at Nina.

Her heart turned over, seeing the way Cleveland defended her. She could see that Addison had inherited his father's charm. "Addison and I have set the date for first Saturday in December," she explained to Cleveland, with whom she felt comfortable. "The Griffiths really have a beautiful home."

"That's wonderful. We will be there. Wouldn't miss it for the world," Cleveland said, his eyes sparkling with warmth.

Oletha's mouth was drawn so tightly that tiny lines appeared around her lips. She sighed with resignation. "Yes, we have to be there. After all, what would people say otherwise?" She made the statement as if it was more a duty than a shared moment of happiness.

Addison placed his arm around Nina's chair and smiled at her encouragingly. "I told you mother would be excited."

Seeing the mischievous glint in his eyes relaxed Nina. She realized that he hadn't expected his mother to be overjoyed about his marriage to her. He squeezed her shoulder affectionately to show her that she was more important to him than his mother's superficial opinion.

* * * * * * * * * * * * *

A few days after the dinner with Addison's parents, Nina received a call at the clinic from Oletha Wagner. "Nina, dear, I called to invite you to lunch. I thought it would be nice for the two of us to get together before the big day."

Nina was stunned by the call and the invitation. "Well, I don't know, Mrs. Wagner. I was planning on eating in. I have some paperwork to do, and . . ."

"I won't take no for an answer," she said. "Surely you can get away for at least an hour. Meet me at the restaurant in the Marriott at about twelve."

Oletha hung up before Nina could say yes or no. She stood and stared at the phone, trying to figure out why Oletha wanted to have lunch with her. She certainly hadn't had much to say the other night—nothing friendly, that is. Nina wanted to call Addison at his office to tell him about her invitation, but decided against it. She knew he had surgery this morning, as well as an office full of patients waiting for him at his private practice. Beside, since Oletha was making an effort to be friendly, Nina saw no harm in meeting her. After all, what could she possibly do to her? Nina mused, returning to the examining room where a patient waited for her.

She arrived at the Marriott restaurant, hoping for the best. She found Oletha Wagner at a corner table, sipping a glass of white wine.

"Sorry I'm late. I had a few last minute phone calls to return to some of my anxious maternity patients," Nina explained, taking a seat in front of the well-dressed, cool, and sophisticated woman. She felt frumpy in the casual black slacks and plain blue shirt she had worn to work. And her sneakers were comfortable, but they certainly weren't fashionable.

"No problem, dear. The most important thing is that you came. Let's order, and then we can talk." Oletha held up her hand to signal for a waitress.

Because Nina was nervous about being alone with Addison's mother, she didn't have much of an appetite. She ordered a chef's salad and a glass of iced tea. Mrs. Wagner ordered the same salad to go along with her wine.

"How are those plans for the wedding?" Oletha folded her manicured hands on the table as though she was at a business meeting.

"Everything is coming right along. Despite a few conflicts with our plans, Kim and I are getting things together." Nina depicted an ease she didn't really feel.

"If you had chosen to have a more formal ceremony, I would have been more than happy to hire a consultant to handle all the details." Oletha's words were loaded with criticism.

A wave of apprehension swept through Nina. "My friend and I are doing fine for the kind of wedding Addison and I want."

The two women fell silent when the waitress appeared to serve their food.

"I have to admit that I am a bit concerned about Addison getting married," said Oletha after they had been served. "I don't believe he has thought this through enough. You two haven't known each other long enough to be rushing into marriage this way."

There it is, Nina thought. There's the real reason for this lunch. "Addison and I aren't teenagers marrying on a whim. We're both mature adults, who realize we have something very special together. We see no sense in waiting. Both of us want to share our lives and to start having a family as soon as we can."

Nina saw Oletha's eyes flash at the mention of their having children, but the older woman did not respond.

The silence was heavy with unspoken tension. Oletha dabbed her mouth like the proper lady she was. She sipped the last of her wine and ordered more, then leaned toward Nina. "You aren't pregnant already, are you? Is that the reason for the hurried ceremony?"

Nina's back went ramrod straight. It hurt her to think Oletha thought her son would marry someone like Nina only if she were carrying his child. She continued to nibble at her salad, hoping that Oletha would change the subject.

"So that's it," Oletha said with finality. "You're tricking him into this marriage. You're after his money and our name. He told me about your grim background, but I thought surely a woman in your profession would have more principles about her than to use a pregnancy to capture a man."

Nina's eyes blazed with anger. "Mrs. Wagner, I only consented to meet you today because I thought you wanted to make up for being so rude to me the other night. But it's obvious you invited me here only to discourage me from marrying your son and joining your precious family."

Mrs. Wagner's lips thinned with irritation. "I want what's best for my son. He's been through one horrendous marriage, and I won't stand by and watch him get hurt again. If it's money you want, I'm prepared to pay you whatever you ask for. I know you're a young physician who is trying to establish herself on her own. I'm quite prepared to give you your price, so that you can pay off your college loans, malpractice insurance, and that little old house of yours. Then you won't have to drag my son into marriage just so you can live like a queen. You can even leave Harper Falls and start anew where no one knows you. It will be our little secret. I promise." She scrutinized Nina, waiting to hear what she clearly hoped for.

There is never an end, Nina thought. Why must the haves always be so hard on the have-nots? she mused, remembering how cruel other people had been to her as she struggled through the foster care system.

"Listen, Mrs. Wagner, I'm not for sale." Nina glared at her with burning, reproachful eyes. "Whether you like it or not, I am going to marry your son. You can choose to accept it, or

174

continue to ignore me and dislike me. It's no big deal to me, as long as I have Addison's love and devotion." She removed her napkin from her lap and laid it on the table, signaling the end of the lunch. "By the way, I'm sure Addison will be very disappointed and hurt by what you've tried to do."

Extreme agitation flashed in Mrs. Wagner's cool eyes. "No! You mustn't say a word to him about this." For a moment her confident demeanor slipped. "If . . . if you do, I'll deny it. You'll only make yourself look like a troublemaker. Surely you wouldn't want to do that before this debacle takes place." She tilted her nose upward and stared at Nina defiantly.

Returning the cold look in the woman's eyes, Nina didn't know whether to despise her or pity her for what she had attempted to do. "I've had enough of this," she replied icily. "I've heard all that I want to from you. I love him, so get over it. I don't care about his money or your precious family name. I really don't understand how you managed to have such a fine man for a son."

Nina jumped to her feet and hurried away from the table and out of the restaurant. Once she was out in the fresh air and sunlight, she felt weak. She wanted to cry. It was humiliating to hear the accusations Addison's mother had made. She realized that if she married Addison, she was going to have to deal with Oletha as long as they were married. Did she have enough love in her heart to deal with such pressure? Was Oletha ever going to accept her—and, most importantly, accept the children who came from her?

Chapter XIV

Leaving Oletha Wagner in the restaurant, Nina headed for Addison's office. She needed to talk about the emotional wringer she had been put through.

Discovering that he had an office full of patients, Nina was about to turn around and leave. She decided that she would talk to him later about what had happened. But just as she was ready to leave, he appeared in the reception area. He welcomed her with a smile and invited her into his office.

"I'm so far behind schedule. But I can take time for you." He sat on the leather sofa in his spacious office and pulled her down beside him. "I had an emergency this morning with one of my patients in the hospital. I haven't even had a chance to go through my mail." He placed his arm around her shoulder. "You're a pleasant sight to see." He kissed her tenderly, holding her to him. "I'm glad you showed up, but what are you doing here? I thought you had those forms to fill out for the clinic."

"I do," she said. "I took time off to have lunch with your mother."

His eyes widened with surprise. "You had lunch with Mother? You didn't mention anything about that last night."

"She called me at work today and invited me. Girl talk," she said. She faltered over the words, her voice weak from turmoil. She wanted to tell him about the awful meeting. Yet she didn't want to be the one to say negative things about the woman he loved and respected.

He studied her intently. "My mother didn't say anything to hurt your feelings, did she? I know she is completely outdone that we won't let her have a hand in planning the ceremony."

Nina hesitated. It took everything in her from telling him the awful things his dear mother had said to her.

The telephone distracted Addison. He lifted it off the receiver before it rang a second time.

"Yes. Sure, she's here. Just a moment." He handed Nina the phone. "It's Rosie from the clinic."

"What is it, Rosie?" Nina asked the receptionist.

"There's a Mrs. Hamilton who has called four times, asking for you. From the number she gave me for you to call, I see that she lives out of the area. She says she has an important message for you."

"I have no idea who she is. Give me the number. I'll call her from here." Nina smiled at Addison and took the pen he'd been using.

"What's that all about?" he asked, watching her dial the number.

"I haven't the slightest idea. But I'll see what's going on soon."

A woman who sounded like a senior citizen answered the phone. "Hello?"

"This is Dr. Sterling in Harper Falls. I'd like to speak with a Mrs. Hamilton."

"Oh, Dr. Sterling, I'm glad you finally called. I'm Mrs. Hamilton," said the woman.

"How can I help you, ma'am?"

"Lord, doctor. She's going to be happy I got you at last."

"Who will be happy?" Nina asked.

"Chloe Martin. She lives down the street from me. She stops over and keeps me company. She's such a sweet child . . ."

Fear knotted inside of Nina. "Uh, Mrs. Hamilton, what about Chloe?"

"Doctor, that little girl needs help. I've been doing my best to help her and her mother, but there is only so much I can do. I'm a widow on a fixed income, you know."

"Mrs. Hamilton, I would love to talk to Chloe or her mother, so that I can find out what's going on. Is there any way you can get Chloe's mother to call me? I will pay the phone charges if you can get them to the phone."

"They live all the way down on the next block. I can't go get them. The arthritis, you know. Chloe came past here this morning to borrow some bread and eggs, and she left your number. She asked me to call you, because she's afraid for her mother." Mrs. Hamilton paused. "That girl's daddy is a mean one. He hangs out with a bad crowd—the ones who do drugs and mess. He beats that poor woman and takes the little money she makes. Then he leaves for days on end. They hardly have food. Chloe said her mother is sick. But I know she is too ashamed to be seen, because he's beat up on her. That goes on too much in front of that baby, doctor."

Squeezing the receiver tightly, Nina shot Addison a look that revealed her anger.

He rose to his feet and stood near her. "What's going on?" he asked in a hushed tone.

178

She held her finger over her lips, instructing him to be quiet. "Could you please tell me where you're calling from and where I can find them to help?" Nina asked.

Mrs. Hamilton chuckled. "I forgot, didn't I? I'm calling from a little old place called Bonney. It's a few hours out of Harper Falls. We live on Percy Street. I live at 118 Percy Street, and Chloe lives in the next block at number 215. You got that, dear?"

"Yes, I have it," Nina said, scribbling on one of Addison's prescription pads. "I'll be there as soon as I can get away. Please help them as best you can. I'll see to it that you're repaid for all you've done. And thanks for the call." Nina hung up. Fury coursed through her.

"It's about Chloe, isn't it?" Addison asked, resting a comforting hand on her shoulder.

"That fool is at it again. He hasn't changed. This lady, Mrs. Hamilton, says that Chloe and her mother don't even have food. She knows that Earl is a mean son of a gun as well. She's seen the bruises on Jenny. From what I gathered, Earl is off on one of his drug binges. Chloe asked her to call me. They need me, Addison."

He took the prescription pad that Nina had written on and read the information.

"That's a two hour drive, Nina," he said. "There's no way I can leave now. You've seen my reception room."

"I have some patients to check on as well," Nina said. "Oh, that poor child."

Thinking about Chloe without any food and possibly without utilities as well, Nina's heart ached. She pictured the little girl helpless and frightened by Earl's irrational behavior and her mother's condition. Such an awful situation for a child to be entangled in, she thought. Tears of frustration spilled from her eyes, and she sobbed softly.

Addison pulled her into the circle of his arms and held her. "It's going to be okay," he said. He cupped her chin and tilted her face toward his. "Let's finish off what we have to do and drive to Bonney this evening. Let's meet at your place about seven."

Nina hugged him to show how grateful she was to have a man like him.

* * * * * * * * * * * * * *

Time crawled for Nina. It seemed like forever before she was able to leave the clinic and head for home. At seven o'clock, Addison called to say he would be on his way as soon as he changed clothes.

Nina prayed that Chloe and Jenny would be safe until she and Addison arrived. She also hoped that Earl would stay out of the way. Surely, Jenny would now be willing to return with Chloe to Harper Falls and live with Nina. Hopefully, this was the wake-up call Jenny needed to make the final break from Earl.

Nina fidgeted about her house, trying to kill time and relax. She watered her plants; she dusted off the painting, "The Birthday Girl," that she'd bought at the African-American Festival a few months ago. She studied the picture, feeling a twinge of melancholy. The painting reminded her of her life as a child with her parents. After all this time, she still remembered the wonderful things they had done as a family. She remembered how her parents had doted on her and how much they'd loved her. She wished that they could meet the man she'd fallen in love with and planned to marry. She believed that they would have adored him as much as she did. She touched the painting and gazed at it as if she were really seeing her parents. "I won't be lonely any more. I'll have my own family soon," she said softly. Emotions welled up in her throat. "I've missed you both so much."

The doorbell rang. Nina shook her head to rid herself of the bittersweet yet precious memories and headed for the door.

Opening the door, she found Jenny and Chloe. "Nina, I'm glad you're home," Jenny exclaimed, falling on Nina to embrace her. She burst into tears.

Silent Chloe wrapped her arms around Nina's leg.

"My goodness, how did you get here?" Nina asked, bringing them in from the chill of the November night and closing the door. "I got Mrs. Hamilton's call today. Addison and I had made plans to come for you tonight." She ushered them into the living room.

"Mrs. Hamilton lent me enough money for bus fare here," Jenny said, following Nina. "She's . . . she's wonderful."

Nina hadn't had a chance to really look at Jenny until she tugged away the hood of her coat, which hid her face. Fury sizzled in Nina's veins at the sight of the dark bruises on each side of her friend's face. She needed no explanation. She knew that Earl had been up to his old tricks. It took everything in her to keep from saying *I told you so.*

"I'm so ashamed to have you see me like this again," Jenny said. "I feel like such a loser." She sighed and lowered her head. "He . . . he was threatening to take Chloe. He wants to hurt me. He blames me for all his problems, Nina. I can't take it anymore. He's gotten worse, not better, in spite of all his promises." Her voice quivered. "When he threatened to take Chloe and sell her to some people who wanted a daughter, I knew I had to leave. Those drugs have turned his mind to mush. He went off with some of his drug friends somewhere. I figured it was the best time for Chloe and me to leave."

"I'm glad you came." Nina knelt to Chloe's eye level. The little girl's big brown eyes, which once had been lively and revealed her zest for life, now held fear. In the time that she had been away, there was no doubt in Nina's mind that this poor child had seen and heard more than she should have. Nina managed a smile for her, hoping she'd match it. "Chloe, baby," she said. "You're safe with me. Everything will be okay." She hugged her. "I've missed you so much, sweetheart. Go into the kitchen and get some cookies and milk like you used to. I've kept your favorite cookies on hand, hoping you'd show up to visit me."

"Go on, Chloe. I'll be in with you soon," Jenny said, turning the reluctant child toward Nina's kitchen.

It broke Nina's heart to see Chloe go slouching off for her snack. The normally loquacious and vivacious child hadn't even said hello to her.

"What's this mess about selling Chloe?" Nina asked when she was sure Chloe couldn't hear.

"The junkies—especially young girls—have been selling their babies and kids, from a thousand dollars on up, to support their habits."

Nina stared in shock. It horrified her to hear such a thing. "Good heavens! What is this world coming to?" she exclaimed.

"In the area where we were living, there was a guy who set up such deals. Earl hasn't worked but one good week since I left Harper Falls with him. He knows how important Chloe is to me. He also resents the fact that the older Chloe gets, the more she looks and acts like her daddy, Willie. He sees that, and he hates it. You'd think Willie was living with us, the way he goes off sometimes. He throws in my face the romance he thinks I had with Willie, all angry and envious. He accuses me of not giving him the kind of love I used to give Chloe's daddy. I *have* tried to love Earl. I've done all I could to help him. It's never enough—never enough!" She sobbed. "I can't take any more."

Nina heard the front door open. She'd left it unlocked for Addison. She assumed it was him, arriving to take her to Chloe. She was glad he'd come. He would be a big help in getting Jenny and Chloe relaxed enough to make plans for a life without Earl.

"I knew this would be the first place you'd come, stupid," Earl growled.

Jenny and Nina jumped at the sound of Earl's menacing voice.

"Get out!" Nina stood in front of Jenny. "You're not welcome in my house." Watching Earl walk toward her and Jenny, Nina noticed how widely dilated his pupils were—a sure sign that he was high.

"I'm not going anywhere until I take my family with me." He glared at Nina. "Jenny, get the girl. Let's go," he ordered loudly.

Jenny stood behind Nina, sniffling. She held onto Nina's shoulders to support her quivering body.

"They're not going with you," Nina announced firmly. "They're staying with me."

Earl staggered toward Nina, scowling at her. "I've had it up to here with you and your high and mighty airs. You can't run my life." He slapped Nina, sending her reeling to the floor.

"Aunt Nina!" Chloe came rushing out of the kitchen to Nina's side.

Earl grabbed Jenny by her collar. "C'mon. Move your stupid tail. I don't have time for this foolishness. You belong with me. You're my woman."

Nina bounded from the floor, wrenched Earl's hands from Jenny's collar, and stepped between the two of them. She refused to be bullied.

Earl seized Nina by the shoulder and drew back his hand to hit her again.

"I'll break your neck if you touch her." Addison stood in the doorway. His handsome face was dark with rage.

Earl swore loudly at Addison's appearance. He shoved Nina away.

"What's going on, Nina?" Addison asked, keeping his eyes on Earl.

"He's been brutalizing Jenny and abusing drugs again," Nina said, moving over to Addison. "Jenny and Chloe came here to get away from him."

Addison's glance fell on Jenny's bruised face, then he swung his gaze to Chloe. He bent and held open his arms to the little girl he had come to adore as much as Nina did.

As Chloe dashed for him, Earl snagged her by the elbow, lifted her, and tucked her under his arm. "You can have that worthless tramp. The child is going with me," he announced with venom. He started backing out of the house.

Addison's eyes flashed with indignation and he stepped toward Earl. "No she isn't."

"Oops, you'd better be careful, doc." With his free hand, Earl pulled out a gun that was jammed inside the front of his jeans and aimed it at Addison.

Nina let out a frightened gasp.

Jenny sobbed. "Earl, please. Don't take Chloe . . . I'll go with you. I'll do anything you want . . . Don't take my baby away." She stepped cautiously toward Earl. "Put that gun away. These are good people. They're just trying to help . . ."

"Shut up! The girl's going with me." Beads of perspiration stood out on Earl's face, which was twisted into an evil grimace.

Chloe began to cry and struggle against Earl to free herself.

Addison made a calculated step toward Earl.

Earl laughed wickedly. "C'mon, doc. Do me a favor, man. I've been wanting you for a long time." He aimed the gun at Addison. "There's nothing I'd like better than to do away with you, with your big-shot ways." A terrible, hot grin tattooed his face.

Nina's blood ran cold at the choices Earl gave them. She couldn't bear the thought of Chloe being taken away by this paranoid maniac. But she couldn't cope with the idea that Addison might be hurt by this monster.

"Forget all of you. You won't run my life," Earl spat, holding onto Chloe and backing out the front door and into the night.

Addison swore. "He's not leaving here with her." He dashed out the door.

Nina's heart stopped with fear. She rushed to the door with Jenny trailing behind, mumbling nervously.

Addison lunged for Earl, knocking him to the ground. He let out a shout and dropped Chloe and his gun.

"Chloe, come here!" Nina screamed to the dazed child, meeting her halfway.

Addison and Earl tumbled and rolled in Nina's front yard. Addison slammed punches into Earl's face.

"Jenny, go call the police. Now!" Nina ordered. She shoved Chloe toward her mother. Nina's eyes were on the gun that lay near the struggling men.

Despite Addison's hard punches, Earl didn't seem to be weakening. He managed to throw a powerful blow to Addison's chin, which caused him to fall away from the other man. Earl rolled over, jumped to his feet, and stomped Addison's groin.

Cursing, Addison doubled up in pain.

Earl scooped the gun off the ground.

Nina rushed up to Earl and grabbed his arm as he swung the gun toward Addison, who was still struggling to get to his feet.

"Let go, woman! Turn me loose now!" Earl cried. He elbowed Nina in the stomach.

She winced in pain, but she clung tightly to his arm to keep him from firing the gun. Struggling against her, he screamed at her and managed to slip a mighty lick to her face.

She dug her nails into his face and raked it, drawing blood. Stunned by the pain, Earl reeled back. He slapped his injured face with his hand and glared at her. "I hate you, b#@*#! You can't keep them from me!" He aimed the gun at her, ready to fire.

Addison had finally regained his feet. He fell on Earl, knocking him to the ground. Once again they rolled on the lawn, fighting and panting. The gun went off twice. The two men froze in their battle.

Nina screamed. As she crept toward the still forms, two police cars with flashing blue lights drove up. The officers hopped out of their cars with their weapons drawn and ordered Nina to step back.

Fear coursed through her; she prayed that Addison hadn't been the one who was injured.

"Addison!" Not heeding the police warning, she ran toward him and dropped to her knees beside his still body. Relief flooded through her when he opened his arms to her and pulled her against his heaving chest. He was panting from exhaustion.

"What a piece of garbage," he muttered, looking toward Earl.

Writhing in pain, Earl lay moaning and clutching his leg. One bullet had gone through his kneecap.

Nina breathed a sigh of relief. "Serves him right."

Chapter XV

"Aunt Nina, you look like a fairy-tale princess," gushed Chloe in awe when she glimpsed Nina in her white satin and lace bridal gown.

"Thank you, sweetheart." Nina smiled. Her brown eyes twinkled at her little angel. "You are beautiful, too. You could be a princess yourself." She admired Chloe's pink flower girl gown with matching satin ribbons streaming from her salon-styled, curly hair.

Kimberly eased up beside Nina and made motherly adjustments to her gown, then smoothed her hair tenderly. She moved around behind her to make sure that everything hung the way it was supposed to.

"I can't believe this day is here," Kimberly said. "You don't know how long I've waited to see you get married." She beamed at Nina. "You are breathtaking. Simply gorgeous." She hugged Nina, being careful not to ruin her hair or make-up. "I'm so happy for you." Her voice quivered.

"Kim, don't start crying. If you do, you're going to get me started and have me messing up my natural make-up." Nina's eyes misted.

Kimberly dabbed at her eyes with a linen handkerchief. "No more tears until later." She laughed softly. "We've got a big day. Everyone is here from the clinic, and several people from St. Luke's have shown up."

"Have you seen her?" Nina asked nervously. "Addison's mother."

"His father is with him," Kimberly said.

"He told me nothing could keep him from being his son's best man," Nina said softly.

"Don't worry about Oletha. She'll come around," Kimberly assured her.

"I won't worry. I refuse to let anyone steal my joy. I'll deal with her later—much later." Nina smiled.

Oletha Wagner had been devastated to learn that Addison was marrying Nina. Then the mess with Earl, which had wound up making the local newspaper and television news, had only proved to the older woman that Nina was not fit to be in their family. People with background did not get tangled up with drug dealers, wife batterers, and shoot-outs. Once Oletha had learned that Addison was unharmed, she hadn't spoken to him or shown any interest in their wedding plans.

"There's no need for me to wish you happiness," Jenny said, stepping up to Nina and taking her hand and patting it. "You've got a good, decent man who's going to give you everything you deserve."

"Thank you, Jenny." Nina kissed her on the cheek, leaving behind a smudge of lipstick. "I'm so glad you're one of my bridesmaids."

"You've made me so happy by asking me to be in your

wedding party. Thank you for being my friend—my sister." Jenny's voice was husky with emotion. She embraced Nina.

When Jenny turned away to adjust Chloe's hair ribbons, Nina's heart stirred with emotion. Jenny looked like a completely different woman. The stress and fear were gone from her face and eyes. Earl was locked up and would be incarcerated for a number of years for the things he had done that night, as well as for other felonies he had committed. Like Nina, Jenny too would have a chance to make a new life for herself and Chloe. Since Nina would be living at Addison's place, she had encouraged Jenny and Chloe to live in her house rent-free.

Amidst the excited chatter and the last-minute grooming adjustments the ladies were making, Nina heard a loud, insistent knocking on Kimberly's bedroom door.

"Ladies," Doug called out from the other side of the door, "you've got to get it together. The minister is here, and it's time to get this show on the road."

"We'll be out soon," said Kimberly. "You wait in the hallway for Nina, honey." She rushed across the room to where the bouquets sat. She handed one to Jenny, and then handed Chloe a white basket with rose petals. "Okay, ladies, let's go. Nina, we'll see you downstairs." She pressed her cheek next to her friend's. "I love you."

After everyone had bustled out, Nina took a deep breath to calm the butterflies in her stomach. She moved to the long, oval-shaped mirror in the corner of the room to get a final glance at herself. She was pleased with what she saw. Love was a wonderful cosmetic, she mused. Her complexion glowed with the love and happiness in her heart on this special day. She was surrounded by friends who loved and cared for her and would be an ultimate lifetime treasure. On this glorious December day, she could finally lay to rest all the insecurities and fears of the "welfare girl," the Nina who had guarded her heart and feelings from a world she'd been left to face alone.

Her only regret was that her parents had not lived to share this moment. Her throat swelled with emotion. Then a warm, comforting feeling enveloped her, and the sadness that was washing over her vanished. Could it be that her parents were with her in spirit, letting her know that they didn't want her to shed any tears of sadness? She smiled at her reflection, wanting to believe that with all her heart. She closed her eyes and placed her hand over her heart where all of her warm memories lived on. "I love you, Daddy and Mommy. You're always with me," she whispered. A tear slid from the corner of each eye.

Kimberly's house resembled an adorable chapel. A profusion of flowers and lighted candles decorated her spacious living room. Guests crowded together, speaking softly while waiting for the ceremony to begin.

Given the signal to begin by Kimberly, the organist hit a sharp chord for Nina's entrance. She appeared on Doug's arm, looking like an angel. They halted at the end of the aisle, as she had been told to do at the rehearsal. Through her veil, she was moved by the pleasant faces looking her way.

As Nina was about to step onto the white tracking, she felt Doug's body stiffen. Glancing his way, she saw the reason for his reaction. Oletha Wagner had slipped in at the last minute.

"Relax, Nina," Doug whispered to her, patting her arm that was looped through his.

Nina eyed the woman, trying to figure out if she had come to ruin everything by letting everyone know that Nina was not welcome in her family.

Oletha's lovely face revealed no emotions.

The organist hit the note again.

"Nina, let's go," Doug urged softly.

"No, not yet," Oletha commanded, stepping to the other side of Nina.

Anxiety as Nina had never known coursed through her. She didn't want any ugly, dramatic scenes to ruin the most important day of her life. She didn't want to hear from this woman that she wasn't good enough for her son. Not today. Not now.

Oletha seized Nina's elbow and leaned near her ear.

Nina lifted her shoulder slightly to discourage the woman.

A slow smile eased the corners of Oletha's mouth. "You are beautiful. I wish you and my son all the best. I *really* do." She stepped away.

Nina stared at Addison's mother, unsure if she had heard her correctly.

"Go on, dear. He's waiting." Oletha waved Nina on.

"C'mon, Nina," Doug said, laughing softly. "Let's not get Oletha mad."

"You're right." Nina sighed. "One . . . two . . . three . . ." She stepped forward, with Doug keeping step to her count. Floating with grace toward the man she loved, she held his adoring gaze. She was buoyed and enchanted by the spirit of the moment.

Standing side by side with Addison before Reverend Kinsey, who spoke in a deep and clear voice, Nina struggled with overwhelming emotions as they exchanged their vows. Addison's eyes sparkled as much as Nina's did with the tears of joy she could no longer hold back.

The minister had barely gotten out the last line of the service when Addison enfolded Nina in his arms and kissed her passionately.

Clinging to her groom, Nina returned the kiss with equal ardor. Her heart sang and her spirits soared. She was truly blessed to know and to share the glory of love—forever and always with Addison, her hero.

Coming Soon...

FALL/WINTER 1997–1998 RELEASES

November 1997

Secret Obsession
Charlene Berry
1-885478-20-8 $10.95

Allysse Dobson has been swept into the fast-paced world of Hollywood producer Wes Hunter. But reality sets in when Wes describes the parameters of their relationship. Unable to accept his terms, Allysse gets involved with Gabe, a firefighter and centerfold model, plunging all three into a whirlpool of secrets, denials, and betrayals.

Also by Charlene Berry, *Love's Deceptions*.

January 1998

Again, My Love
Kayla Perrin
1-885478-23-2 $10.95

Gavin's ultimatum makes Marcia's choice a painful one—her career or him.

Forced to make a decision, Marcia follows her career, leaving Gavin behind but taking with her the pain of parting ways.

Marcia does find love again, and enjoys a great career and then . . . Gavin! After a long absence he decides to claim his first and only love, Marcia!

February 1998

Gentle Yearning
Rochelle Alers
1-885478-24-0 $10.95

Daniel Clinton's affair with his best friend's beautiful widow, Rebecca, yields more than love. Nearly torn apart by guilt and deceit, both yield to their overwhelming desires and love for each other, forever.

     Also by Rochelle Alers, *Careless Whispers* and *Reckless Surrender*.

March 1998

Midnight Peril
Vicki Andrews
1-885478-27-5 $10.95

Leslie, a bright and attractive corporate attorney, is divorced and a single mother of a teenage daughter. Somehow she finds the time to fall in love, but falls for two very different men, before intriguing events and circumstances narrow her love interest to the one man she really needs.

March 1998

Quiet Storm
Donna Hill
1-885478-29-1 $10.95

Deanna is beautiful and immensely talented. As a concert pianist and accomplished equestrian, she is constantly in the public eye touring the world. Many admire, yet envy, her beauty, talent, and relationship with actor Cord Herrera. But in one moment, tragedy casts a dark shadow over Deanna's bright future . . . producing a quiet storm, calmed only by an unexpected liaison.